HIS OWN WAY OUT

TAYLOR SARACEN

HIS OWN WAY OUT

The Rise Up Series
Book One
by
Taylor Saracen

13 Red Media Ltd.

HIS OWN WAY OUT

Photography by Alejandro Palomares

Cover Design by Emily Irwin

Proofreading by The Pro Book Editor

To Blake
May your ambition continue to be as powerful as your dreams, and may your fears be few. My friend, this book is for you.

ACKNOWLEDGMENTS

First and foremost, a big thank you to Keith Miller for understanding and enhancing the vision of this project. Without his belief in me and the series, none of this would be possible. A special thank you to Blake Mitchell for enduring countless phone calls, texts, and emails while I ensured I had this thing right. I'm grateful to know him. To Kyle Ross for his support, positivity, and professionalism. An awed thank you to Emily Irwin for her ability to continuously create art that is more beautiful than I could have imagined. Thank you to Jill Savoia for being my forever go-to in all areas of everything and for her honesty. To Jenifer Friedman for opening my eyes to a world of possibility. Finally, a resounding thank you to my family for their endless love and support in all I do, and for dealing with my highly annoying writing habits without too much ribbing.

HIS OWN WAY OUT

PART I

JUNIOR

1

It should have never happened the way it did, Blake knew that. Unfortunately, knowing something was fucked up didn't magically give him the ability to alter it. No matter how much he wanted to, he couldn't erase the actions of the petty prick who outed him as bisexual. There was no way to go back in time and re-pave the path or stand in the middle of the Woodland County High School hallway with his hands on his hips, chest puffed, strong like Superman, ready to block the trajectory of the truth that was hurled at him, shot beyond him, splattered on the lockers for everyone to see. If he'd been given the opportunity to rewrite his reality, Blake never would have messed around with the mouthy motherfucker. Maybe then he could have evaded the wrath of Xander's rejection, an apparent consequence of the cold shoulder Blake had checked him with.

Although there was nothing he could do to change the past, Blake did have power over the present, but he wasn't sure he gave a shit about it. Sophomore year had been difficult thanks to the unexpected exposure, and he didn't have much hope that junior year would be any kinder.

"Are you ready for this?" Greg Bobash asked, nudging the toe of his sneakers against Blake's knee while he sat on a school step, wishing he was pretty much anywhere else.

"I'm here," he answered, rubbing his palm over the tacky sweat that accumulated on his neck thanks to the brutal late-summer humidity in Kentucky.

"I guess that's a start," Greg teased, taking Blake's hand and pulling him to his feet. "They say half the battle is showing up."

"Who are *they* anyway?" Blake questioned, smirking at his friend. "I bet it's a bunch of people I would never want to hang out with, assholes who say shit like that."

"I just said it."

"You did," Blake confirmed, laughing as Greg bristled at the implication. "You're stuck with me, G."

"I'm not complaining," Greg grinned, patting Blake's shoulder as they crossed the threshold into the new school year.

"You better not be."

Blake couldn't deny that Greg was a strange bird, but his friend had proven he was as solid as stone. While his wrestling teammates had turned their backs on Blake after his unauthorized outing, Greg, and a few other outcasts, hadn't wavered—which was fine with Blake. He had always felt more comfortable with them anyway.

Adjusting the backpack straps on his shoulders, Blake ignored his peers' curious glances as he walked toward his homeroom. Memories of the first day of sophomore year came to mind, and Blake was taken aback by how different it had felt. Back then, there wasn't a foreboding cloud hanging in the mornings. Everything was bright, new, and teeming with possibility. After exclusively attending private schools, Blake thought that transferring to a public school would be easy, and although it was a piece of cake academically, the social aspect was more than he bargained for.

The student population of Woodland High was five times the size of his previous school, which was cool for a while. He liked being around different people and learning new things, but when shit went down with Xander, Blake wished there had been less ears to hear and fewer mouths to spread the news. It was a complete mindfuck to be around more people than ever before, and then deal with the fact that they were wary of him because of the person who he inherently was. It was only natural he'd grown cynical and worried that when he faced the real world after high school, he would contend with the same lack of acceptance, but on a greater scale.

"Welcome back, Mr. Mitchell," Ms. Patton greeted, extending her hand to shake Blake's before he entered the classroom.

"Good morning, ma'am," he replied, looking her straight in the eyes, just as he'd been taught to do since he was little boy.

"Let's make it a good year," she said, a sentiment that was immediately sullied when Blake walked into the room and saw none other than Xander Marks sitting in one of the desks furthest from the teacher's.

As Blake begrudgingly sank into a seat at the front of the room, he silently cursed his father for giving him a last name that began with "M," Xander for being a snake, and Ms. Patton for disproved positivity.

While the rest of his morning was uneventful, Blake found confirmation that his year was bound to be a complete calamity when his ex-girlfriend Claire Kenwood walked into the cafeteria hand-in-hand with a senior Blake didn't recognize. Last year, Blake ended his low-key relationship with Xander to be with Claire, a choice he didn't regret, regardless of how things turned out. If it were up to him, Blake would still be with Claire, but unfortunately, it wasn't. Claire was a good Christian girl with good Christian parents who didn't want her with a not-so-good-Christian bisexual boy.

"You okay?" Greg asked, knocking his knee against Blake's under the table.

"Why wouldn't I be?" he replied, averting his gaze from the girl he wanted to be with to focus on his half-eaten turkey sandwich instead.

"I don't know," Greg tsked as if the answer was obvious, which, if Blake was being honest, it was. "Maybe you wouldn't be because Claire strolled in here with some beast of a football player on her arm, looking cozy."

"I didn't notice."

"Oh," Greg nodded, clearly not buying the bullshit, "you didn't notice?"

"Nope," Blake replied, rolling his lips tight to his teeth while rubbing his thumb over his chin. "Not at all."

The blond took a big bite of his pizza, rolled his eyes and hummed, "Hmm."

"Don't *hmm* me."

"Alright."

"I'm not some pussy," Blake stated matter-of-factly.

Greg lifted his free arm in mock surrender. "Hey, hey, hey. I didn't say you were!"

"I know you didn't say it, but I'm making sure you know it."

The way Greg lifted his pale eyebrows in amusement had Blake cracking a smile despite himself. Though he'd known his friend for less than a year, Blake liked how his boy could read him, even when it was aggravating. It was nice to have someone at school who had his back.

"Got it," Greg assured, holding up his thumb.

"Corny," Blake laughed.

"I prefer husky," Greg corrected, grabbing one of his stomach rolls and giving it a jiggle. "You can't relate."

"Not quite," Blake teased, waggling his eyebrows as he lifted his shirt a bit to flash his taut abs.

"Show off," Greg grinned.

"There's nothing wrong with being proud of your body. Work out with me," he urged. "It'll be fun."

"Fun is getting high and eating Cheetos, not running around chafing my ballsack during the ass-crack of summer."

"Are you offering?" Blake asked, thinking how a bowl was exactly what he needed.

"My sweaty ballsack?"

"Weed, douchebag," Blake chuckled, shaking his head. "We could blaze after school."

"I have a little something," Greg nodded.

"You have a little what?" their friend Ian McManus asked, plopping into the seat beside Greg.

"Pot."

"Ah," the redhead nodded. "I thought you were talking about your dick."

"I have much more dick than I have weed," Greg sighed. "It's a curse."

"I'm sure," Ian laughed. "You got enough for me to join?"

"Yeah."

"Less for us then," Blake pointed out. "You should come with some Budweiser from your dad's stash to even it out."

"It's not even your weed," Ian exclaimed as Blake leaned back in his chair, crossed his arms over his chest, and gave him a shit-eating grin.

"Blake's a businessman," Greg said, clapping Blake's back heartily. "Always out here wheeling and dealing."

"You know me," Blake clicked his tongue, "I have to work that hustle. Are you going to bring the Bud?"

"Are you assholes going to come with me to Matt's party tonight if I do?"

"It's Monday. Who parties on a Monday night?" Greg chided.

"We do, right?" Ian replied, tilting his head in Blake's direction. "Are you in?"

While Blake knew it probably wasn't the best idea to go out and get blasted when he had to be up early for school the next morning, he didn't care. His day had been shitty, and it seemed like doing things differently could steer his year in the right direction. It's not like he had homework beyond getting his syllabuses signed, and he wasn't sure he would give a damn even if he had a report due the next day.

"I'm in," Blake decided, taking the final bite of his sandwich. "This is good."

"Good, huh?" Greg challenged. "I'd call it a lot of things, but I'm not sure good is one of them."

"Bad things can be good sometimes if you do them right," Blake told Greg, laughing when his friend poked his finger into Blake's dimple.

"You're a cheeky one today," Greg noted with a sigh. "I guess I could think of worse things to do. I mean, even the mention of this improved your mood. What kind of friend would I be if I denied you?"

"A boring one," Blake suggested.

"Super boring," Ian agreed. "Don't be a super boring guy, Greg."

"Peer pressure is next level in eleventh grade," the blond observed, tapping his forehead thoughtfully. "Fine, I'll go."

"Good. You're driving," Blake grinned.

"What the fuck?" Greg exclaimed.

"I don't have a license and McManus doesn't have a car, you have both."

"The burden of being a responsible guy," Greg sighed, taking a swig of his Dr. Pepper.

"Truly," Blake agreed, patting his friend's hand. "I plan to avoid the heavy lifting for as long as possible."

"Except for weights. You think it's *fun* to lift those," Greg reminded Blake.

"Not as fun as getting smashed on a school night. I feel like, this year, partying should take priority over..." Blake thought for a moment, "everything. No girls, no boys, no drama, just good old-fashioned debauchery."

"That sounds productive," Greg smirked.

"I like the new Blake," Ian added.

Blake nodded, wondering if he could like the "new Blake," too. Maybe junior year had some potential after all.

By the time Blake, Greg, and Ian made it to Matt's family farm, Blake was so bombed, he knew he had no business being anywhere but in bed sobering up. Still, he persisted, ready to own the night or, at the very least, rent it for the next couple of hours. Even though he was definitely in a better space than earlier that day, he was emotionally exhausted by the wherewithal it took to suffer his peers sober. It could have been worse—earlier that morning his mind had spun with awful scenarios that hadn't materialized—but he couldn't ignore the fact that it could have gone better, too.

The night felt different than the constrained day, like it was full of possibility and opportunities to explore. As was customary for August, the afternoon air was stifling, but the evening offered reprieve. A light breeze tickled Blake's skin with a hint of impending autumn, while the warmth of summer lingered to kiss the apples of his cheeks. It was strange how even a passing glance at the thorny thicket of Kentucky plum trees beyond the stables could spark nostalgia and flood Blake with a contentedness he so rarely experienced anymore. Memories of being a rambunctious, cherub-faced five-year-old and leaping under 'Ivory Silk' trees with his older brother, Logan, flitted into his mind. Blake and Logan would laugh until their sides hurt as they attempted to grab the cream-colored lilacs that hung from the limbs. Eventually they'd tumble into the plush bluegrass and lie on their backs to watch butterflies and hummingbirds flutter to the fragrant blooms. Things were never simple, not even then, but Blake had thought they were, which was as good as it being so.

While Blake was aware that seventeen wasn't exactly old, he'd never thought of himself as young. Adult responsibilities had seeped into the years meant to be marked by youthful giggles and skinned knees. It wasn't as though he hadn't had a happy childhood, it was more that he'd always thought he was grown and should be treated accordingly—so sometimes he was. It was a stark contrast from his more recent desire to shirk all obligation.

"Earth to Blake," Ian sang, elbowing Blake in the rib cage playfully. "Do you have a craving for some plums, man? Are you looking to keep yourself regular on that geriatric shit?"

"Dumbass," Blake chided, reaching into the back pocket of Ian's jeans to lift the cigarettes they'd gone half on earlier. "The only thing I'm craving is nicotine."

"And chemicals, carcinogens, toxins, tar, carbon monoxide, formaldehyde, ammonia, cyanide, arsenic, DDT..." Greg added, clicking his tongue in disapproval as Blake placed the paper between his lips and cupped his hands to light it up.

"Yeah, well, I don't think the resin in your bowl, the beers we pounded, and the gas station burritos we ate for dinner are doing anything to keep us in optimal health," he retorted, waving Ian off when he tried to high-five him. "It is a bad habit."

But it was one Blake had not yet had the capacity to quit. He blamed Dominic. Though, if he was being honest, he held his mom's boyfriend responsible for a lot of things the guy may not have actually been guilty of. Dom was an easy scapegoat, being far from an angel himself. Regardless of whether Dominic deserved the blame about other things, it was him who gave Blake his first cigarette at twelve, so the smoking was at least partially on him. Maybe Blake and Dominic were too similar or too painfully different. Either way, things had rarely worked between them, and that was alright with Blake. There were many things to dislike about Dom, but his redeeming qualities made it difficult for Blake to despise him. It had been tough for Blake to be away from his mom when she was diagnosed with cancer during his freshman year at boarding school, but there was some solace in knowing that Dominic had stepped up to care for her. When Blake decided to come back to Unionville for sophomore year and enroll in public school rather than being away, Dom and Logan told him that things were fine. Still, it didn't feel right to be states away when his mother was sick. Though she had other people there for her, he wanted to be one of them, too.

"We all have bad habits," Greg stated as they pushed past the crowd of revelers surrounding the keg, "some worse than others, but at the end of the day, we're all fucked up. It's all about who hides it better. Speaking of being fucked up," he continued, pushing his palm against his eye sockets, "I'm like ninety-five percent wasted off my ass."

"I'm glad you drove our asses out to east bumblefuck on the remaining five," Blake tsked. "And you're giving me shit for doing dumb stuff, hmm?"

"You weren't complaining when your ass didn't have to walk here," Greg reminded, "Saint Blake."

"Saint Blake," Blake laughed, grabbing a red solo cup from the haystacks they were stacked on. "I didn't realize Catholics were down with me."

"I'm down with you," Ian grinned.

"The king of Catholics over here," Greg teased, grabbing his friend's sides.

"The Pope," Ian corrected, taking Blake's cup so he could fill it up.

"That's all head," Blake said, watching froth accumulate.

"When have you ever complained about too much head?" Greg joked.

"Fair," Blake smirked, dumping the contents of his cup into the dirt behind him, only to adjust the angle and tap the keg again. "It's been a while. I'm giving myself tendonitis."

"Welcome to the Virgin Club, we wear wrist braces to sleep."

"I don't qualify for your club," Blake assured them, turning around to scan the people gathered close to the keg. Though he'd decided relationship drama had to be avoided at all costs, he couldn't help but think a good fuck was just what he needed to clear his already inebriated mind. "Haven't been a member for three years."

"Show off," Greg huffed, taking a swig of his beer.

"It's easier for him," Ian reasoned. "I mean, he'll bang guys and girls. He has an increased probability of sinking his dick in."

"I wish," Blake sighed with a click of his tongue. It wasn't that easy. He was definitely able to score some ass, but he spent more time jacking off than he did pounding into someone's body. That's what he needed, the ultimate release. "I'm going to go check out the cabin," he decided, observing a sea of people as they undulated in.

"I thought you were avoiding drama. 'New year, new Blake,'" Greg said, repeating Blake's mantra from earlier in the afternoon.

"Well, I never said 'new Blake' wouldn't get laid," Blake smiled. "I'm all for self-flagellation, but only within reason."

Sipping his beer as he shuffled between groups of people, Blake headed toward the house, figuring he would know who he was looking for when he found them. There were significantly more kids in attendance than just those who went to his school, which was good for Blake. He had a better chance of getting ass if he was getting it from someone he didn't know, someone who didn't know him.

Saying "excuse me" as he weaved through the football players who were congregating on the porch stairs, Blake was forced to stop in his tracks when one of them turned around and stood like a boulder on the step above him, hands on his hips, clearly intending to deny Blake access.

"Really?" Blake sighed, perturbed.

"What's the password?" the boulder asked, looking quite proud of himself for being a prick.

"Move?"

"That's not it," he answered, shaking his head. "Try again."

If Blake was a fighter, he would have been compelled to throw a punch, but he wasn't. He had watched Logan go that way for a while, and he wasn't about it, but that didn't mean he was afraid to talk shit once in a while.

"I think it's 'fuck off' then," Blake replied, pursing his lips and sniffing in annoyance. "So, fuck off."

As expected, the statement rubbed the boulder the wrong way, and Blake closed his eyes, bracing for the impact that didn't come.

"C'mon Dyson, let him through," another guy urged, garnering a side-eye from Blake. It was the football player Claire had walked into the cafeteria with earlier that day. Blake was aware that it was a pretty stand-up thing for him to do, but he wasn't interested in his charity.

The boulder listened, and Blake pushed past him, entering the residence with the chip—that he thought he'd ditched—firmly back on his shoulder. Though the cabin was spacious, there was barely any room to move. He squeezed through smoke-hazed hallways following the smell of weed. He could use another hit. Draining his cup in an attempt to cool his rapidly overheating body, Blake practically fell into a small room full of guys he recognized from P.E.

"Hey Mitchell," Nick Holgate greeted, giving Blake a slight nod as he continued to cut lines on the coffee table in the middle of the group. "You want in?"

"Uh, no." Blake replied, leaning against the wall in an attempt to stop the room from spinning.

"Your loss," Nate shrugged, slipping his license back into his wallet.

Blake doubted it. He had no interest in cocaine. To him, the drug was as useless as the beater trucks douchebags had lined up on the field outside the cabin. Though the bodies of the pickups were deteriorating, they had been tricked out with expensive sound systems which their owners had worked the whole summer to pay for. The guys showed off their rides like they were whipping out their cocks, trying to prove whose was bigger. Blake was pretty sure, even without a car, that his had them all beat.

"It's a good high," Jack Heismore said, looking back at Blake from where he was kneeling on the ground.

"Yeah?"

"Mmmhmm," Jack confirmed.

"It makes you feel like Superman," Nick added, pointing at the graphic on Blake's t-shirt. "You sure you don't want to give it a try, Superman? See if it makes you soar?"

Licking his lips, Blake said, "I'm good," even though he wasn't sure he was. The last beer he'd chugged had him lapping the threshold to utter intoxication he had passed hours before, and then jogging back to demolish it completely.

He needed to get away. Giving the guys a wordless wave, he ventured back into the hallway, somehow stumbling onto the mostly empty back deck. Lying on the wood plank bench, Blake stared up at the reverberating stars, wondering when they had become so active. He would wait for Greg to come and find him. Until then, he'd close his eyes.

Blake woke on Tuesday morning feeling like death. Three hours of sleep, a throbbing head, and a churning stomach had him thinking "new Blake" was an idiot. Although "old Blake" had made a slew of questionable decisions, he hadn't been as remorseful over them as he was the prior night's final cup of beer.

Stretching his arms over his head, Blake groaned as his muscles lengthened. He wiped the sleep out of his eyes before putting on his glasses and grabbing his phone from his nightstand.

Blake (6:12am): Pick me up on your way to school.

Greg (6:13am): You're not on my way

Blake (6:15am): I'm a half a mile past it.

Greg (6:15am): I know, that's why you walk

Blake (6:16am): It'll take you an extra two minutes.

Greg (6:16am): Somebody's feeling rough this morning I see...

Blake (6:16am): Understatement.

Greg (6:17am): You were in rare form

Blake (6:17am): I don't want to know.

Greg (6:18am): lmao then I can't wait to tell you

Blake (6:18am): Great. Tell me when you pick me up.

Greg (6:19am): You're persuasive

Blake (6:19am): So I hear.
Greg (6:19am): I'll be there but you're buying me shit at Circle K
Blake (6:20am): Whatever.

Tossing his phone onto the comforter, Blake climbed out of bed, tottering a bit as he let out a massive yawn.

"Fuck," he murmured, plodding to the bathroom.

Blake placed his glasses on the counter, intent on making it through his morning routine without puking. Standing under the stream of the shower head, he wet his body and turned to rest his forehead against the cool tiles of the stall. He allowed the hot water to pelt his back for longer than usual, hoping it would dissolve the tension in his traps. He had to get it together, and not in the half-assed way he'd vowed to the day before. The last thing he wanted to do was become some lush who drank his life away. He wanted wrestling to start stat. Just the thought of hitting the mat lifted his spirits slightly. Instead of fucking around, he needed to buckle down and get into top shape for the season. He knew he could accomplish a lot in two months if he was focused. That's what he would look forward to—wrestling. He had a good run last season, but good wasn't enough. He wanted to be great. He wanted to win the Woodland Invitational and then head to States. Winners didn't drink booze for dinner and party all night.

Feeling at least partially renewed, he toweled off and put on his usual uniform of a t-shirt, jeans, and Wildcat snapback.

"I'm surprised you're up," Logan said as Blake took a seat across from him at the kitchen table. "You were in rough shape last night."

"So I hear," Blake grumbled, grimacing as egg yolk dripped down his brother's chin. "Ugh. Wipe your face."

Logan rolled his eyes and picked up his napkin. "What did you do to mom?"

"What do you mean?" Blake asked averting his eyes, even watching Logan chew was making him nauseous.

"If I ever got home two hours past curfew she'd have my ass. When you do she's getting you Tylenol and making sure you have water by your bed."

Blake shrugged. It was true. He was the baby and his mom treated him that way, catering to him more than she did Logan. Blake didn't get away with as much as Logan liked to pretend he did, but he couldn't deny that he had the ability to talk himself out of things that would've had his brother on lockdown.

Logan shook his head, getting up to drop his plate in the sink.

"Rinse it off and put it in the dishwasher," Grace Mitchell directed her eldest son as she entered the kitchen.

"Do you tell Blake to do the same?" Logan asked, raising his dark eyebrows as if he already knew the answer.

"Constantly," she assured, kissing Logan's cheek. "Right, Blake?"

"Yup," Blake confirmed, clearing his throat as he dumped a bottle of Gatorade into his backpack. Suddenly he was compelled to get out of the house as quickly as possible. He didn't have the energy to listen to a lecture about how he was "letting himself down."

"You're in a hurry," Grace noted, standing behind Blake with her hands on her hips. "What's the rush?"

"I don't want to be late for school."

"Oh, you don't want to be late for school," she said in an over exaggerated tone. "And here I thought you'd forgotten how to tell time."

"He probably did last night since he was stupid drunk," Logan interjected, earning an unimpressed middle finger from Blake.

"Hey," his mom chided, smacking his hand down without much force, "quit it." She sighed. "First of all, you overdid whatever you did last night. It's unacceptable and I won't stand for it. Second, you were out far beyond your curfew and you had me worried sick."

"I know," Blake nodded. "I'm sorry. I shouldn't have gone out at all. I got wrapped up in," he paused, not wanting to admit that he struggled through the first day of school, "the excitement of the new year and everything."

Logan made a point to roll his eyes at the comment, but Blake ignored him, knowing that if he looked at his mother softly, he'd be off the hook.

"You're better than this, Blake," Grace reminded him, pushing a loose wave off of his forehead. "When you do stuff like this you aren't only letting me down, you're letting yourself down."

Blake inhaled deeply and punched out a remorseful sigh. His mother repeated the sentiment often, and it never ceased to hit him to the heart each time. He didn't want to disappoint his mom. It wasn't as if Blake was ignorant to the fact that some of the things he did were messed up. So much of him wanted to grow up and stop doing stupid teenage shit altogether, but the opportunity to have fun and be free of restrictions was too tempting a pull to resist. He knew he needed to try harder.

"Life's easier when you do the right thing," Grace said, resting her hand on Blake's face tenderly. "Listen to me when I tell you that. You know I speak from experience."

"Okay, mom," Blake said, well aware that she did.

Though his mother hadn't always made choices that Blake easily understood, it was apparent to him, even at a young age, that she learned from every victory and each mistake. She wanted to do better, to *be* better, in the same way she hoped for him. It was easier to buy into a mantra of cyclical self-improvement when it was modeled instead of preached.

She patted his cheek, tightening her lips before admitting, "I hope you do."

It was difficult for Blake to see that she wavered in her trust of him, but he had given her a fair amount of reasons to have doubts.

He sniffed and let out a lion yawn. It was too early in the morning to deal with the mélange of emotions.

"Cover your mouth," she tsked, turning to Logan. "I correct him too."

"Mm-hmm," he hummed, sounding thoroughly unconvinced.

A short series of beeps from the driveway had Blake hurrying out the door, disregarding Logan's request that they wait for him. His brother was too whiny to deal with on top of his splitting headache.

"Good morning, Sunshine!" Greg exclaimed loudly as soon as Blake opened the passenger door of the Ford Focus. "You look like you've been run over by a tractor, but you're still oddly attractive."

"I don't even know," Blake laughed lightly, shaking his head, "I don't even know how to respond to that."

"Say 'thank you.' It's a compliment to your good looks," Greg grinned, making the volume on the radio louder as he backed out onto the street. "Handsome bastard."

"Turn it down," Blake ordered.

"The radio or my voice?"

"Both, actually."

"Remember when I told you on our third beer that we should skip Matt's party?"

Blake closed his eyes and tilted his heavy head back. "Vaguely."

"What did you say in return?" Greg pressed.

"Probably that you were a bitch?" Blake ventured.

"You got it. Who's the bitch now, Mitchell?"

"Still you," Blake smirked, huffing when Greg smacked his arm. "Ouch."

"There's no way you felt that past those muscles," Greg stated. "Oh shit." He started to dance in his seat. "My song."

When Greg proceeded to belt out Carly Rae Jepson's "Call Me Maybe," Blake considered throwing himself out of the car, wondering if he would survive the tuck and roll without any broken bones. After a moment's deliberation, he decided it wasn't worth risking the wrestling season.

"You're doing this to annoy me," Blake said matter-of-factly, glaring at his friend.

"No, I'm doing this to punish you for keeping me out until three in the morning," Greg corrected with a grin. "Your third-wind was epic. Do you want to hear about it?"

"Nope."

"The dancing?"

"No."

"The kissing?"

Blake raised an interested eyebrow.

"I'm just fucking with you. The only thing you kissed was your knees while you tried not to puke in the backseat of my car."

"And I was successful?" Blake asked hopefully, cringing when Greg gestured to the pile of towels on the backseat. "I'll buy your lunch, too."

"Deal, but you're cleaning it."

"Yeah, I know," Blake sighed. "Was I really dancing?"

"Nah. You were too shitfaced to embarrass yourself."

"I'm a good dancer."

"Whatever you have to tell yourself."

"You've never even seen me dance," Blake argued, wondering why he was engaging in the conversation at all. Somehow, the meaningless banter was keeping his mind away from his flipping stomach, so he went with it. "I have rhythm. Ask anyone I've fucked."

Very deliberately, Greg reached for Blake's hand and leaned in close to talk to his palm. "Does Blake have rhythm?"

"Fuck you," Blake laughed.

It had been a while.

"I'm going big for breakfast," Greg said as he pulled into the Circle K parking lot. "Prepare your wallet."

"It's ready," Blake replied. "I expected it."

"That's why I love you, Mitchell. You're smart."

"I do dumb shit."

"So stop doing dumb shit," Greg said easily, as they walked into the convenience store. "You can stop, can't you?"

"Of course I can," Blake answered, not entirely convinced.

All he knew was that he had to try.

4

It was impressive what Blake could achieve in a couple of months when he was lucid and driven. While he still partied with Greg and Ian, or Nick Holgate and his crew on the weekends, he was serious on school days. Aside from working out every afternoon, he was eating right and going to bed at a reasonable hour. Blake had spoken to his guidance counselor about enrolling in the cooperative program Woodland County High had with a vocational school in Lexington. Thanks to his sophomore year grades and participation on the wrestling team, he was accepted past the initial registration date. Getting out of Unionville for half of the day was a breath of fresh air. Although his time was spent in another school, and not hanging around the city like he would have wanted, it was liberating.

Not only did Blake appreciate the change of scenery, he also enjoyed the program in which he had enrolled. He'd always been interested in law enforcement, and the Homeland Security curriculum seemed to be a good fit. Even though he didn't put a ton of thought into future career options—figuring it out was something he could worry about in college—Blake did like the idea of having a job that varied depending on the assignment. With

ADHD, it was difficult to be stuck in the same cycle. He needed movement and action, something more than the mundane nine to five.

"Are you going to the wrestling meeting today?" Steve Cook asked Blake as they exited their classroom and walked toward the bus following the morning session at the Lexington Institute of Technology.

Steve had been inquiring about Blake's intentions regarding wrestling for the last few weeks. He wondered if Steve broached the topic because he had nothing else to talk to him about. If that was the case, Blake would have much preferred if his classmate didn't speak to him at all. While he didn't have anything against Steve, they didn't really have much in common besides their shared interests in the Homeland Security program and wrestling. It would've been enough to elicit conversation with other people, but the way Steve approached topics made Blake uncomfortable. He was so blunt that it came off as abrasive.

"Yup," Blake answered coolly, sliding his hands into the pockets of his jeans. "I'll be there."

"Coach will probably hand out information packets and stuff."

"Sounds about right."

"That's what he does every year and it's always the same information."

"Hmm," Blake nodded, wishing Steve could read social cues. It would have been quite obvious to anyone who was tuned in that Blake wasn't interested in chatting.

"Last year was your first year at WCHS, right? So, you've only had to sit through the meeting once before. I've done it twice. This will be my third time."

"Yeah."

As they climbed onto the bus, Blake hoped Steve would sit with a friend of his who was in the welding program, but unfortunately, he had no such luck. Pulling his hat low on his face, Blake tucked his chin to his chest and closed his eyes, hoping his intention to be left alone would be clear. It wasn't.

"So, are you looking forward to it?" Steve asked, popping gum into his mouth and offering Blake a piece.

"No thanks," he said, sighing out his aggravation and pinching the bridge of his nose under his frames. "Am I looking forward to what?"

"To wrestling season."

"Oh. Yeah," Blake nodded, edging as close to the bus window as he could get. "I'm going to nap."

"Right now?"

"Right now."

"Can you sleep with all the noise?" Steve asked surprised.

Very deliberately, Blake grabbed earbuds from his backpack and put them in, letting music fill his ears rather than Steve's inane comments. Gazing out the window at the lush green landscape and picturesque farms, he imagined what it would be like to see the ocean instead, something so immense and mysterious, different from the same dips and hills he'd seen so many times before. Sometimes he had to remind himself that there was a whole world beyond the Kentucky state lines, a world where things would perhaps be better for him, where he would be understood.

By the time the bus pulled into the Woodland County High School parking lot, Blake was more ready than ever for the wrestling season to begin. Maybe if he did well and made it to State, he could get on a recruiters' radar and have the opportunity to earn a scholarship to a D1 school. Just the thought of what his future may hold spiked his confidence. He walked into the school with a swagger he hadn't mustered since he transferred to the public school the year prior.

As soon as Blake entered the building, he caught sight of Claire and two of her friends standing outside the library. They were smiling and laughing, books held tight against their chests as they caught up on the latest gossip. She was beautiful. He hadn't allowed himself to really look at her since things had gone so wrong months before. Led by a surge of self-assuredness, Blake popped the buds out of his ears and approached the small circle of girls.

"Hey," he greeted, his eyes locked on Claire's, making it obvious he was there for one reason.

"Hi," she replied tucking her straight brown hair behind her ears, unable to conceal how surprised she was by his presence.

"Can I talk to you for a minute?" Blake asked, noticing the shock on Claire's friends' faces. He wondered how often he'd been a topic of conversation. He hoped it was a lot.

"Okay," she nodded, following him down the hallway a bit. "How are you?"

"How do I look?" he replied, grinning when her cheeks tinged pink. It was good to see he still drew the reaction.

"You know what I mean," Claire tsked, the slightest hint of a smile turning up the corners of her pink pout. "How's everything?"

"Everything's good," Blake answered easily. "I've been thinking about a lot lately."

"That must be good for your grades," she grinned.

"Yeah, and good for you, too."

"Why's that?" Claire asked, clearly humoring him.

"Because I have a masterplan."

"A masterplan?" she repeated, amusement dancing across her sky-blue eyes. "What does that have to do with me?"

"Everything," Blake said matter-of-factly. He moved closer to her, able to hear the way her breath stuttered at his proximity. He knew what got her, what drove her crazy, and the way she was biting her lower lip made him glad it was still him.

She didn't ask another question, backing away from the heat instead. While Blake was aware that Claire had a boyfriend, he didn't really care. Things had been good between them before all the shit with Xander went down, and Blake wanted them to be that way again. It was unfathomable that his sexual orientation could impact her family so significantly, especially when it was one part out of the thousands he was made of. Had they forgotten about his sense of humor, respectful manner, and every other positive quality that they seemed to admire less than a year ago?

Blake watched Claire rejoin her friends, giving her a mischievous smirk when she glanced over her shoulder at him.

The swagger he'd acquired a few moments earlier was laced with a content pep in his step. He didn't have a masterplan, but if he had he was positive that getting Claire worked up like he had, was number one on the list. He put a mental check mark next to phase one.

With excitement about his interaction with Claire and the promise of wrestling season at the forefront of his mind, the remainder of the school day was pleasant. For the first time in a long time, things were headed in the right direction. The surge of positivity made it possible for Blake to overlook the cliquey vibe in the classroom where the wrestling meeting was held. The guys on the team had always been tight, so it wasn't a surprise. They'd all grown up together, their lives bound to Unionville in a way that Blake's never was. It had been challenging to be an outsider, but grew used to it after a while.

"Welcome back, guys," Coach Lowery said, his voice low and gruff despite the sentiment of his statement. "I'm not going to keep you here for longer than you need to be since you all know the drill. Take a packet, get a physical, have your parents sign the permission slips if you're under eighteen, and show up at tryouts prepared to bust your asses to make the team. I don't care who you are, if you don't bring it, you'll get cut."

Blake nodded, knowing he was primed to compete. He'd managed to build more muscle over the last month than he had over the course of the season the year before. He was strong and ready.

Coach clapped. "That's it, get out of here."

The classroom filled with the buzz of conversation as the guys walked to the back of the room to grab the paperwork.

"Hey Blake. What's good?" Andre Jackson asked, reaching out his hand to shake Blake's.

"Everything," he grinned. It wasn't a lie. "How are you?"

"Doing good, man. Are you thinking about joining up this year?"

"Yup," Blake replied, amused by how obvious the answer was. "I'm here, so..."

"Yeah," Andre nodded, "You are."

They looked at each other for an awkward moment before Blake glanced away.

"What about you..." Blake began. "Are you thinking about it?"

"Yeah," Andre answered, clicking his tongue. "Yeah, yeah."

"Got it."

Blake nodded his head along with Andre's, wondering why they were standing there like bumbling bobble-heads.

"I'll see you on the mat then," Blake said finally, putting a period on the bizarre exchange.

"See you there," Andre said.

Blake could feel Andre's eyes on him as he picked up the paperwork. Between Steve and Andre, Blake was convinced the team was full of fucking weirdos, which was alright. He was kind of weird, too.

5

Drinking with Nick was more of a disparate experience than partying with Greg and Ian. While Greg typically remained coherent enough to look out for Blake, Nick was often just as far gone, if not more. The result was either that Blake would police himself better, or he would eagerly go into an alcohol-steeped abyss with his friend. The nearer wrestling season drew, the more responsible Blake had become when going out with Nick on the weekends. He found it even more imperative that he keep it under control after Coach's informational meeting. Things were gearing up and he wanted to be ready for tryouts.

"I'm going to go outside," Blake told Nick as his buddy crowded the keg alongside a bunch of other kids from school. Gemma Green's basement was dark and dank, and the sheer number of people packed into it had Blake feeling claustrophobic.

When Nick asked him earlier that day if he wanted to hit up the party, Blake thought it was a good idea, but he found it hard to get into the mood.

"Do you," Nick shrugged, patting Blake on the back before swiveling to talk to a girl that was in Blake's health class. The expression on her face was a clear indication that—try as he may—Nick wasn't getting laid.

Blake had never been around a guy as good looking as Nick who got rejected so often. He was aware that his friend's personality wasn't for everyone, but he didn't find it as off-putting as the girl Nick tried to hit on did. While Blake definitely had some room to grow in the game department, he was an all-star player compared to Nick, a fact that he found both perplexing and awesome. A few times, Blake had attempted to observe exactly where things went wrong for Nick in his quest to get pussy, but there wasn't one thing he could pinpoint as the issue. He made girls uncomfortable, and not in the intriguing bad-boy way. It was more a smarmy you-know-what-I-want-from-you vibe. Blake liked sex, and he didn't mind leading with it when he was getting to know someone, but he was in-tune enough with people's energy to recognize when shit wasn't working. Nick wasn't.

Walking onto the porch, Blake took a seat in an oversized Adirondack chair, lit up a cigarette and took a drag. After a deep inhale he let out a longer exhale, watching as a grey plume of smoke snaked up toward the star-filled sky. The October air was crisp, but the alcohol that had settled in his stomach kept him warm. The parties he attended were always the same—cabins, barns, farms and kegs— but somehow, every night managed to feel different. Perhaps it was because he was different. So easily affected by his emotions that his temperament skewed the way he saw things, how he reacted. At times, he was driven to remain on the surface, not delving deeper into his feelings, accepting the world around him as it was. Mostly, though, he got caught in his head, too meta about the intricacies of social relationships and how he fit in—or didn't. His penchant for elevated cognition could have been attributed to the amount of weed he'd smoked prior to leaving Nick's house. The nights Blake found himself locked in his head often began with bongs and bowls. It was better that way. He liked to think deeper, to exist on a higher plane of consciousness, hang out above the minutia of the day.

"Can I bum one off of you?" a guy asked, sitting in the chair beside Blake's. Though the size of the furniture kept them far apart,

Blake could smell the soap and beer on the boy he didn't recognize. Somehow, when mixed with the stranger's full lips and handsome face, the common combination of scents was intoxicating.

"Uh, yeah, sure," Blake replied, reaching for the pack he'd placed on his arm before lounging. He held it out to him and licked his lips as the guy rested the filter on his.

"The lighter too?" the boy directed with a slight grin.

Blake passed him the BIC and admired the length and gracefulness of the guy's fingers as he flicked the wheel.

"Thanks," he grinned, returning the items to Blake before settling back in the chair.

"No problem," Blake said, tapping his toes in his sneakers as he tried to decide what to say. "You don't go to Woodland, do you?"

He shook his head. "Nah, I go to a private school up in Lexington. You go to Woodland?"

Blake nodded. "Yeah.

"How do you like it?"

"It's alright," Blake answered easily. "It's school, so I don't know. It's okay."

"You're not into school?"

Shrugging, Blake tapped his ash. "I don't *not* like it, I guess. I think it's the level of obligation that gets me. The lack of freedom."

"I can see that," he contemplated, thoughtfully. "I like to learn but I feel the same. That's why I'm looking forward to college next year."

"You're a senior?"

"Yeah. How about you?" he asked, as the reflection of the festoon lights strung on the parapet danced across his gentle brown eyes.

"I'm a junior."

"You look older," he commented.

Blake grinned, assuming it was a compliment. "Do you know where you're going to go?"

"Hmm?"

"For college," Blake clarified. "Do you have applications out and stuff?"

"Oh," he laughed at his obtuseness, "sorry I'm buzzing. I do. I'm waiting to hear back from a few schools, especially UK."

"Nice." Blake couldn't help but be attracted to his ambition and his arms. He could see the outline of his muscles under the thin grey Henley he was wearing. "Good luck with that."

"Thanks," he paused as if he was waiting for Blake to fill in his name.

"Blake."

"Thanks, Blake," he said. "I'm Rider."

"Rider," Blake repeated, liking the way the name sounded on his tongue. He wanted Rider on his tongue.

"That's me," Rider smirked.

The fleeting moment of flirtation was all Blake needed. Confidently, he extended his left leg, nudging Rider's foot with his own.

Rider bit his lower lip. An invitation. Blake wanted him, wanted to get lost in the moment, to sink into someone else, escape himself.

"C'mon," Blake said, dropping his cigarette so he could stomp it out. He stood up and gestured for Rider to follow him down the stairs, his heart pounding as he did.

Blake led the older boy to the edge of the corn fields, placing a hand on Rider's narrow waist as he leaned in for a kiss. Rider reacted how Blake hoped he would, parting his lips to slide his tongue along the inside of Blake's cheek. Tumbling into the tangle, Blake worked his tongue around Rider's, slow, seductive circles. He grunted when Rider slid his hands in Blake's back pockets and pulled him in closer.

As the kiss intensified, Blake slid one hand up Rider's shirt to feel the definition of his abs, while the other dropped to the bulge in Rider's jeans. Wrapping his hand around Rider, Blake began to stroke him on top of his pants, moaning softly at the sounds of Rider's groans.

"I don't do shit with guys," Rider whispered breathlessly as Blake sucked on his neck.

Blake peeled his lips off Rider's smooth skin. "Does your dick know that?" he asked, continuing to work him. "It seems like it has other ideas."

"What I want and what I need are two different things," Rider said, placing his palm on Blake's cheek in a way that felt like goodbye. "Fuck, you're cute."

"And you're confused," Blake replied. "Who *needs* anything at eighteen? It's all about wants. When are we ever going to be led by our wants again?"

Rider sighed, slotting their mouths together for another kiss. "Okay, okay, okay," he chanted, backing away. He rubbed his forehead as he punched out a stuttering exhale. "I'm fucked up."

"On drugs or repression?"

"Both, probably," Rider admitted.

The last thing Blake was interested in was dealing with a guy with a guilt problem, no matter how hot he was.

Rider's reluctance was obvious as he pulled away. "I should go."

"Okay," Blake said, noticing the pang of disappointment in Rider's eyes. Maybe he wanted Blake to fight for him, at least for the night, but he didn't have the energy. Everything shouldn't need to be a struggle. "You're missing out, you know," Blake called after Rider as he made his way back to the house.

"Believe me, I know," Rider assured Blake as he checked him out.

"Not on me," he amended. "Well maybe on me, but on life. You're missing out on life, pretending to be someone you're not."

"You don't?"

"I don't what?"

"Pretend to be something you're not."

Though there was distance between them, Blake could see the trepidation in Rider's eyes.

"Not anymore. At least I try not to," Blake answered, shaking his head for emphasis.

"And how's that working out for you?" Rider asked genuinely. It was odd that a guy who seemingly had his shit together was interested in hearing Blake's thoughts.

"I have no idea," Blake confessed, unable to hold back his laughter. "Every day is different."

"Well, you give me hope, Blake, because for me, every day is exactly the same."

"I hope you get into Kentucky and find some change."

"And I hope you don't change at all," Rider decided. It looked as if he was going to close the gap between them, but instead his feet remained planted in the dirt.

"You don't know me," Blake reminded, the sincerity in Rider's statement taking him aback.

"I know enough to know you shouldn't."

And with that, Rider gave Blake a wave and turned to head back to the party. Blake watched as he took the steps by twos and disappeared into the house to pretend to be someone he wasn't. He wondered how many people stood under the same roof wishing they weren't who they were.

Lying down on the cold ground, Blake gazed up at the moon, thinking of how the moment would have been poignant if he hadn't been left in a corn field with balls as blue as his eyes.

6

As expected, wrestling tryouts had gone well for Blake and he had no problem making the team. Not only had his performance caused a surge in his self-worth, but the mere act of being on the mat had elevated his mood, which was already improving by the day. He was in a good place, probably the best that he'd been in since he transferred to WCHS, and he didn't take that for granted.

"Look at you," Grace exclaimed when she came into the kitchen to find Blake scrambling eggs and frying bacon.

Turning over his shoulder, he grinned at his mom, gesturing toward the toaster. "I'm making toast, too. Do you want me to fix you a plate?"

"To what do we owe this pleasure?" Logan asked, grabbing a piece of bacon out of the pan. "Ouch!" he yelped when Blake swatted his ass with the wooden spoon he'd been using on the eggs. "What the fuck? You got my pants dirty, you prick!"

"I offered breakfast to Mom, not you. I didn't make enough to feed your big mouth."

"He can have mine," Grace decided, kissing Blake on the cheek. "I need to get to work."

"You're missing out," Blake said in a sing-song tone.

"I'll be the judge of that," Logan interjected, taking a seat at the table and tapping his fingers as though Blake's preparation was taking too long.

Grace clicked her tongue and shuffled out of the room just as Dominic was coming in.

"How was work?" she asked her boyfriend, who was clearly beat after his overnight shift at the gas station.

"It was work, Grace," he said as if her obvious attempt at pleasantry was completely missed.

"I'll see you later," Grace said, ignoring the edge in his voice. "Bye boys."

Blake waved goodbye and glanced at Dom. "Do you want some breakfast?"

"I could eat," Dominic nodded.

"Fucking asshole," Logan scoffed, looking slightly amused by Blake's pettiness.

"You already had a piece of bacon," Blake defended. "That should hold you over."

"Did I steal your breakfast?" Dominic asked, seemingly less concerned when Blake dropped a plate of food in front of him. He dug in immediately.

"Since when do you do nice shit for Dom anyway? You only gave him breakfast to piss me off," Logan pointed out as if Blake's motivation weren't glaringly apparent.

"Is that true?" Dominic questioned, his mouth full of eggs.

"Yup," Blake confirmed as he took a bite of his bacon.

Dom shrugged. "I'm not above eating spite food."

"Nobody ever thought you would be," Logan huffed, standing up to get a slice of cheese out of the refrigerator.

"Have you actually given thought to that, Lo? Like, you've sat around and wondered if you would eat food that was given strictly to aggravate another person? That's popped into your head often enough to have formed an opinion on Dom's position?"

"Honestly, Blake, you're so annoying that I wouldn't want to eat your food and risk becoming an asshole by proxy," Logan stated, before leaving the room.

"You really made him mad," Dom noted.

"I did," Blake agreed.

"And here I am reaping the rewards. You know, you're not a shitty cook. You should do it more often, especially for me."

"Yeah," Blake pursed his lips. "That's not gonna happen. Enjoy the meal, it's your last."

"That sounds like a threat," Dominic stated, nonplussed.

Blake laughed. "It came out more sinister than I meant it."

"You've always been a little boring. I thought things were about to get interesting," Dom grinned, lifting an eyebrow.

"Sorry to disappoint," Blake said offhandedly, taking his plate to the sink to rinse it off.

It never ceased to be unnerving that Blake couldn't read Dominic. With other people, he could determine a cause and effect relationship to their actions or words, but with Dom, there was only impulse. When he was younger, Blake thought Dom's unpredictability was cool. He liked that he never knew what was going to come out of his mouth, until the shit that did was undercutting. Almost seven years later, like it or not, Blake had grown somewhat used to not being used to Dominic.

"Grace said you made the wrestling team," Dominic began, instantly interrupting himself— "Get me some orange juice."

Blake figured it was an improvement that Dominic had shown interest for a split second. It was hard not to compare Dominic to others in fatherly roles, although it was a position Dominic neither wanted nor deserved. While Blake's actual father was very much a rolling stone, he was invested in a way no other man Grace had been with could be, and that was fine with Blake.

"Please," Blake prompted as if he was training a child in the simplest show of politeness.

"Please," Dom repeated, belching a "thank you" when Blake handed him a glass.

Every one of Dominic's bad habits made Blake want to be better. He was oddly inspiring.

"I'm leaving," Blake announced, deciding he didn't want to spend another moment with the guy. His first practice of the season was later that day and he didn't want things to be dampened by additional time with Dom.

"Break a leg," Dom called as Blake exited the house.

He didn't have the energy to tell the asshole that the phrase wasn't used in sports for obvious reasons. Placing his headphones in his ears, Blake walked to school, got on the bus to Lexington, and didn't remove the buds until he was sitting at his table in Homeland Security.

"How was your weekend?" Steve asked, placing his book on the table as he sat down in his usual spot beside Blake.

"Fine. How about yours?"

Monday mornings were typically exhausting, but they were made more so when they were spent with Steve.

"Good," his classmate replied, licking his thin lips as if he was priming his mouth to ask a question.

Blake regarded Steve expectantly for a moment before glancing away, hoping that when he looked back again things would be less awkward.

"Can I ask you a question?" Steve ventured, which was strange on its own accord considering the guy asked him a never-ending succession of questions daily.

There it was. After a few months of being forced to hang around with Steve, Blake had gained the ability to read his cues, even when Steve was too obtuse to have honed the same skill.

"I guess," Blake answered, hoping it was something he felt apt to handle at eight in the morning.

"Are you gay?"

The question hung in the air between them, as invasive as it was inappropriate. Blake knew he didn't have to reveal any pieces of himself to Steve, but he had made a decision last year—after the

Xander shit went down—not to pretend to be something, or someone, he wasn't.

"No," Blake replied, noticing how a look of relief washed over Steve's acne scarred face.

Relief. A guy who had no stake in Blake's life whatsoever was *relieved* to hear he wasn't gay, something that would never impact him in the least.

"I'm bi," Blake continued, watching the relief shift to confusion. He had no idea how a teenager in 2012 could not know what bi meant. "Bisexual," he clarified. "I'm into guys and girls."

"Oh," Steve nodded his understanding. "That's still kind of gay though, right? I mean, if you're into guys...that's gay."

Though Blake truly wanted to tell the guy off for being so ignorant, he decided an attempt at educating him was a better course of action.

"It would make me gay if I was only into guys, but since I'm also into girls, it makes me bi."

"It's the being into guys part that bothers the rest of the team," Steve stated. "I mean, the fact that you're into dudes at all..." He paused as if contemplating how to make what he was saying less shitty. "They don't want you to wrestle with us."

Blake stared at the de facto dickhead of a spokesman in utter disbelief. There was no doubt in his mind that the team had put Steve up to the conversation because they knew he was dense enough to go along with it. They didn't want him on the team. They didn't want to wrestle with him. Shaking his head, Blake attempted to grab onto any of the words that were frenetically popping into his head but was unable to settle on anything that had enough weight. Instead of a full retort, Blake simply said, "Well, it's not up to them," because it wasn't.

"All I'm saying is they don't want to wrestle you in practice and stuff in case you get, like, turned on by it or whatever," Steve added, as if the sentiment made shit any better. "We wouldn't have a girl on the squad, you know?"

"That's so stupid," Blake spat as the anger boiling in his blood heated his face. "You dumbasses should be more worried about the fact that I'm going to be a beast this year, who devours everyone before I crush State."

"You can only do that if people are willing to wrestle you," Steve reminded, his voice lacking the hostility that would have married well with the malicious statement.

Too flabbergasted to say anything else, Blake seethed for the remainder of the morning and then some more when he got back to Woodland. There was no chance he was going to let a bunch of homophobic, biphobic ingrates run him off the team. They had some nerve putting Steve up to the task, but they would have to face him themselves. What a bunch of pussies. After months of looking forward to wrestling, he was determined not to let the bullshit bother him, but he had no idea how to ignore something so absurdly wrong. Regardless of how much he wanted to forget that Steve had said anything, Blake knew there was no way to easily purge the feelings of rage and hurt he was experiencing.

And just like that, Blake was dreading the practice he'd been looking forward to for weeks.

7

S howing up to practice took more nerve than Blake expected. The stress pressing on his chest was similar to what he'd experienced when he faced his peers after Xander outed him, but somehow it managed to be exponentially worse knowing that people were so disgusted by him that they didn't want him to participate in a sport they all loved. He should have been angrier than he was, should have allowed himself to be driven by their fear. In theory, their hate should have spurred him to be better, to excel in a way they couldn't because they didn't need to rise after being pushed down. It was easy to imagine walking into the room and telling them all to go fuck themselves before absolutely wrecking them on the mat, but actually entering a room full of people who didn't want him there wore on him more than he would have liked.

Blake stood among the team, *his* team, attempting to hear past the sound of his heart pounding in his ears as Coach gave his instructions. Although Blake knew that he needed to calm down, he couldn't. The deep breaths he attempted to draw to slow the pace of his pulse were too shallow to settle it down. The last thing he needed was to pass out. Clearing his throat, Blake took a sip of his water, trying to cover the erratic pants escaping his lips. He had to get it together. Their opinions shouldn't have meant anything. They were nothing more than a bunch of ignorant fucks who were most likely living their glory years, with nowhere else to go but down. They'd live and die in Unionville or some other small town where they'd spout off shit about valuing their neighbors while being assholes to anyone who was different from them.

"Alright," Coach said, ending the speech Blake hadn't been able to pay attention to, "Pair up."

It was immediate, every guy quickly found a partner while Blake stood on his own, odd man out. Though he wanted to lay Steve out, Blake found himself wishing the squirrelly motherfucker would've thrown him a goddamn nut and teamed up with him.

"We'll cycle you in, Mitchell," Coach Lowery said, and Blake wondered if the older man knew why he was sitting alone on the bench. If he did, he didn't show any sign of correcting the team's behavior. He was probably like them anyway. It was delusional to expect more. There would have been a modicum or vindication, but it wasn't like having Coach read the team the riot act would make Blake feel any less like a leper. In fact, it would probably make things worse, if that were possible.

Thirty minutes passed, and Blake's ass was firmly planted on the bench as nary a teammate glanced in his direction. He'd never felt more seen and ignored in his life. On wobbly knees, he walked over to Coach Lowery, intent on participating even if he wasn't wanted.

"Coach," Blake said, cursing his voice for cracking with stress. "I'm ready to get out there. Do you want to pair me up?"

"Uh, yeah, sure," he said watching the boys on the mat. "How about you go in for DePandy?" He cupped his hands around his mouth. "Hey DePandy, take a breather. Lakin, you have Mitchell."

"I gotta take a leak, Coach," Tyler Lakin said nervously. "Jeremiah can take Blake."

"Fine by me," Coach Lowery huffed, unaffected by the brush off.

"Why don't you take Mitchell when you get back from the bathroom?" Jeremiah Burbar suggested, shifting uncomfortably. "I'm already winded."

Coach Lowery narrowed his eyes. "If that's the case you shouldn't have made the team, Jer. Stay in, work on your stamina."

Jeremiah nudged his knuckle against his nose as Blake joined him on the mat. "Don't try any funny business," Jeremiah warned, the statement taking Blake aback.

"Funny business," he repeated, "like telling fucking jokes? Don't worry, man, I take this shit seriously."

"That's not what I meant," Jeremiah said as if Blake hadn't gotten the message clearly.

Blake rolled his eyes and got low, ready to practice the skills he'd observed the team working on for the last half hour.

"Watch your hands," Jeremiah chided, standing up to shove Blake after being pinned to the ground.

"Learn to wrestle," Blake retorted, jaw clenched. "That was regulation take down."

"There's nothing regulation about you," the senior snarled, as the venom in his voice sank into Blake's skin.

"Fucking dick," Blake scoffed, shaking his head as he eyed down the douchebag.

"I figured you'd call me a dick. It's what you got on your mind, right?"

"Clever," Blake muttered, trying to hide that the statement had knocked the air out of his lungs.

"Any other compliments?" Jeremiah challenged.

Blake shook his head. "Can't think of one."

With that, Blake started to walk, sure that it wasn't the right decision, however, he was painfully aware that he could only take so much, and he knew he was nearing capacity. As much as he knew he would regret fucking off, he knew he'd regret staying for further berating a lot more.

After a quick change, Blake began the three-mile trek to the only place it made sense to go.

"I thought you had practice today," Greg said, as he opened the front door to let Blake in.

"Yeah, that didn't go so well," Blake replied, dropping his bag in the foyer and following his friend up to his bedroom. "Got any weed?"

"You know I do," Greg nodded, turning back to grin at Blake. "You look pissed."

"I am pissed."

"What happened?"

"I'll tell you after you pack the bowl," Blake sighed, lying back on Greg's bed and draping his forearm over his face.

"Did you fart or something?" Greg asked. "Like bust ass while a dude had you in a hold?"

Despite himself, Blake chuckled. "That would have been less mortifying."

"Did you shit yourself?"

Sitting up to glare at Greg, Blake uttered, "No, I didn't shit myself, dumbass."

"What happened then?" Greg pressed, handing Blake the pipe and lighter.

"Nobody wanted to practice with me. Like, they were doing anything they could not to go near me."

"Because of that stuff Steve brought up this morning?"

Blake nodded, placing his lips on the glass to draw the marijuana deep into his lungs. Closing his eyes, he let the smoke fuzzy his mind, making the events of the afternoon feel like they were a million miles away.

"Did you tell them that you have good taste and that you wouldn't be into any of them because they're budget beefcakes with fucked up faces?" Greg inquired, reaching for the weed.

Clapping his hand over his mouth to stifle his laughter, Blake shook his head. "Nah, I think I missed the boat on that one."

"There's always tomorrow."

"I don't know about that."

"What the fuck, Blake!" Greg cried. "You're not going to quit the team. That's what they want. You show up tomorrow, and the next day, and the day after that with fucking bells on. Not only because you love wrestling, but in spite of them. Let this bullshit inspire you to be better than every single last one of those motherfuckers."

"This isn't an after-school special, G."

"I know. If it was, I'd be six-feet-tall and cut."

"Eh," Blake shrugged. "The best friend is usually a little chubby."

Greg laughed. "Fuck you. The hero is usually charming."

"I'm charming as fuck."

"I'm not charmed by you right now," Greg stated. "You called me chubby." The fake pout on his friend's face had Blake chuckling again.

"I said, 'a little chubby,'" Blake clarified. "Pleasantly plump."

"Tool," Greg tsked. He shook his head and sighed. "Seriously though, you have to stick with it, man. They'll get over it eventually and if they don't, fuck them."

"I don't want to fuck them," Blake reminded, with a yawn. "Whatever. I don't want to think about it right now. I want to get blazed and then get wasted enough that I won't know what day it is."

"But it will still be Monday. Remember we're off the Monday, Tuesday, Wednesday, Thursday thing."

"Remember what I told you went down an hour ago?" Blake challenged. The last thing he needed was for Greg to pull some saint shit when he wanted to get obliterated.

"I do. You should go workout or something. Get out some of your aggression and get better than the rest of them," Greg suggested.

"I'm already better than them."

"Well, get better than better."

"That doesn't exist," Blake chided. "Are we going out or what?"

Greg shook his head. "I don't think so. I'll kickback with you here but I don't want to get sloppy on a school night. I learned my lesson a few months ago. I thought you did, too."

Blake rolled his eyes. "When shitty things happen, you're allowed to go out and get shitty and not feel shitty about it."

"I think that's shitty reasoning."

"Whatever," Blake grumbled, taking another hit. Pulling his phone out of his pocket, he shot off a text to Nick.

Blake (5:17pm): Do you wanna get fucked up tonight?

Nick (5:18pm): When have I ever said no to
that question?

Nick (5:18pm): What are you thinking?

Blake (5:19pm): Do you think one of your boys in Lexington would know of something going on up there?

Nick (5:22pm): Doing it big on a Monday. I love it.

Blake (5:22pm): Knew you would. I'm at Greg's. Tell me what's up and I'll meet you at the bus stop when you wanna roll.

Nick (5:24pm): I'm on it.

While Blake was well aware that heading up to Lexington with Nick wasn't the best idea, he was also damn positive that he didn't give a shit. He needed to blow-off steam and couldn't think of a better way to do it. Maybe he'd feel different about things the next day, or maybe he wouldn't feel anything. He liked that option better.

8
_____

Even though Blake had been hungover as hell, he'd dragged himself to the second wrestling practice, and when the same bullshit ensued, he decided that he wasn't going to go back for the third. A person could only cope with so much ostracization and Blake had reached his capacity. If the team's rejection hadn't made him feel bad enough, his own shame over quitting had been the icing on the disgrace cake. So, he spent the next several weeks drowning his pain in copious amounts of alcohol and sobering up just enough to get high and go to school. The constant state of inebriation made it tolerable to pass the assholes on the team in the hallways, but it did nothing to help Blake survive Steve at the table they shared every morning. Luckily, the king of being socially inappropriate and daft seemed to recognize that things were awkward as fuck between them and didn't attempt to engage Blake in a lot of conversation.

The more time he devoted to getting fucked up, the less he was with Greg, who definitely wasn't a fan of his reckless behavior. Blake knew his friend was looking out for him, but it got old to hear Greg make the same points ad nauseam when all Blake wanted to do was think of nothing but where the party was that night.

"It's hard to watch you practically pass out on the table, man," Greg sighed, nudging Blake's bicep as he buried his face in his forearms. The cafeteria was so damn bright, and his head was throbbing too intensely to hold it up and deal with the fluorescent lighting.

"I'm not passing out, dick. It's Day-Glo in here. It's bothering my eyes."

"That's because you're hungover. You look rough, Blake."

Blake could hear the tenderness in Greg's tone. He kept his head down, not only because of his migraine, but because he didn't want to see the worry that had become a permanent fixture on his friend's face.

"Don't look at me then," Blake grumbled, knowing it was a fucked-up thing to say as soon as the words came out of his mouth. He should have attempted to reel them back in, but he was tired, and he wouldn't have minded some quiet, even if it meant he was sitting alone. There were worse things to be than by yourself anyway.

"I'm going to ignore that one," Greg said. He'd been turning a deaf ear to a lot of shit Blake had been saying, not budging regardless of how hard Blake pushed him away. Blake wondered what it would be like to be a sturdy rock like Greg, rather than a rushing river like himself. Greg was solid and steadfast, while Blake was impacted by the elements, weak while he waited for rain and dangerous when he couldn't manage it. He wished he was less erratic, or that Greg was more so. Maybe then they wouldn't have felt so far apart.

"You shouldn't," Blake murmured. "One of these days you won't."

"Is that your plan? To push me away? Be so insufferable that I fuck off?"

Blake didn't reply, instead he listened to Greg's wry laugh.

"Have you met my parents?"

The question was rhetorical. Of course he had.

"If I can put up with those lunatics on the daily, I can surely deal with your bitch ass," Greg stated.

Blake wanted to hug him. He wanted to tell him that he was glad to have a friend like him in his corner. He wanted to thank him, but instead he kicked Greg's foot with the toe of his sneaker, it was all the affection he could muster.

"You know what we should do over winter break?" Greg began, a clear attempt to lighten the mood.

"Bong hits?" Blake proposed, lifting his head enough to give Greg a small grin.

"Other than that. We should workout. Go to the gym or throw bags of rice and tires around. Whatever the fuck you like to do."

The suggestion was enough to have Blake sitting up fully. "You want to work out with me?"

"Sure. Doesn't every fatty make a New Year's resolution to get in shape? I'm just a lucky chunk with a best friend who looks like you," Greg replied easily. "It makes sense that I'd exploit your talents for my own gain, doesn't it?"

"I get what you're trying to do."

"And...?" Greg shrugged.

"And it's a valiant effort."

"One that will work?"

"That's up in the air," Blake replied, "but fuck if I'm not impressed that you're willing to risk life and limb to try."

"Life and limb," Greg chuckled. "Do you really think I'm that out of shape that I'd keel over if I worked out with you?"

"Maybe," Blake grinned, resting his head on his friend's shoulder. "I like you even if you annoy me. I don't want to kill you."

"That's the sweetest thing you've said to me in a long time, Mitchell," Greg said, ruffling Blake's hair. "I'm suddenly feeling soft toward you."

"You're always feeling soft toward me."

"Is that a fat kid joke?"

Blake clicked his tongue and took off his glasses, so he could rub his eyes. "Not at all."

"You two are goals," Ian remarked from across the table, barely glancing up from his phone.

"I don't know about that," Greg remarked. "I gotta put in a lot of work for this cuddly outcome."

"But it's worth it," Blake teased.

"Definitely worth it," Greg confirmed, petting Blake's head again.

"Faggots," Jeremiah Burbar scoffed as he walked past the table.

"Really?" Blake growled, as a sudden charge of energy woke up his tired body.

"Not worth it," Greg said quickly, resting his hand on Blake's shoulder.

"Definitely not worth it," Ian confirmed. "That piece of trash is going to live a miserable life with a wife who hates him and two ugly kids who cry all the time."

"You've put a strange amount of thought into this, haven't you?" Greg asked, pursing his lips as he regarded Ian skeptically.

Ian shrugged.

"Like what, do you see in my future? Are you a psychic now?" Greg continued. "Should I ask you the lottery numbers?"

"You're not eighteen yet," Blake said.

"And you're not twenty-one but that doesn't stop you from drinking on the regular," Greg chided. "Let me win the lottery in peace."

"Fuck, he's such a douchebag," Blake sighed unable to move beyond Jeremiah's bullshit. It was crazy to think that there were more Jeremiahs around than Gregs. If the world were full of Gregs, there wouldn't be any homophobia, biphobia, racism, or sexism. All Blake wanted was a land of Gregs, but it seemed he was stuck in a school full of Jeremiahs.

"Don't let him bother you," Greg tsked. "I know it's easier said than done."

"Much," Blake agreed, pushing his glasses up on his nose.

The blaring bell made Blake cringe as he slowly climbed to his feet, throwing his backpack over his shoulders. Four more classes; he only had to make it through four more classes before winter break would officially commence. Though he'd been treating the last couple of months like a party, Blake was glad to not have to wake up early.

Ambling through the hallway, Blake kept his head down, feeling as though it was too heavy to lift.

"Hi," Claire said, her sweet southern drawl easy on Blake's irritated ears. She was walking beside him, progress he would have been happy about a few weeks prior.

"Hey," he muttered, barely looking at her.

She smelled like vanilla and clove, a scent that instantly reminded Blake of how sweet she tasted, how much he loved kissing her, and how the simple act of placing his lips on her earlobes drove her absolutely crazy.

"Are you ready for break?" she asked, an attempt at small talk. He didn't want small talk. He didn't want any talking. He wanted kissing, her hands on his body, and for her to break up with her boyfriend.

"Yeah," he answered coolly. He didn't have the energy to fight for her, to compete with some dude who was probably as big an asshole as Jeremiah, Steve and the rest of the fools on the wrestling team. If she wanted to be with a guy like that, she could have him.

They walked wordlessly, a wall of awkwardness erected between them.

"Are you alright?" Claire inquired, clearly uncomfortable with the silence. "You don't look so good."

Blake huffed out a sardonic laugh.

"You know what I mean," she admonished with a sigh. "It seems like you have something on your mind."

"I do," Blake stated matter-of-factly. "Is this your way of asking if it's you?"

Her cheeks tinted pink, and for a split-second Blake considered kissing them.

"I guess I'm worried about you," she admitted. "Every week you've just seemed, I don't know, sadder."

"You've been watching me."

"You're hard to ignore."

"You've done a pretty good job for the last year," Blake reminded, drawing a tsk from Claire.

"That's not fair."

"You're right, it isn't," Blake agreed, positive they were each referencing different infractions.

"Have a Merry Christmas, Blake," Claire said, appearing to be exasperated by the conversation.

He watched as she walked away, muttering under his breath, "You, too."

Blake imagined how quaint Christmas was in the Kenwood house. They probably wore matching pajamas and woke up at the crack of dawn. They would gather around a huge, shimmering tree to open their loads of presents. Claire's Mom would make banana pancakes and hot chocolate and they would enjoy the meal while snuggling up under flannel blankets and watching "A Charlie Brown Christmas." It would snow outside their house, but only a light dusting, which ensured perfect photo opportunities for the family in their Fair Isle sweaters. Claire didn't have a Dominic or a Mom who had to bust her ass to put food on the table. She didn't have to shovel the three feet of snow that would likely fall on Blake, or fight with her siblings over dumb shit.

Claire's life was perfect, and Blake wasn't. It was easy to understand why he was no longer a part of it, even if it sucked.

9

The Woodland County Invitational was a big deal. The annual wrestling tournament took place a few days before Christmas and people all over the county showed up to cheer the competitors on. Wrestlers from neighboring high schools trained just as hard as the WCHS boys did, because the overall winner typically had a great chance at repeating the achievement at State. Blake had thought he would be participating, that he would win, that he would then be headed to State to do the same. Instead, he was sitting in his bedroom, getting high with Nick, wondering why the weed wasn't settling his mind like it usually did.

The sound of the garage door opening had Blake cracking the window and frantically waving as much of the smoke out of the room as he could.

"Shit," he grunted, grabbing the bowl from Nick in order to pour a few drops of water on the embers.

"Are you serious right now?" Nick exclaimed, wide eyes vacillating from the now soggy contents of the pipe to Blake. "You just fucked up perfectly good weed."

"Yeah, well, my mom's home and she'll have my ass if she catches me smoking," Blake said lighting the cranberry and fern candle he'd lifted from the living room.

"She's not gonna think it's shady as shit that we're sitting up here in the middle of the afternoon channeling some romance?" Nick laughed.

"I mean, think about it," Blake smirked. "She would be less fazed by the chance that we were banging than she would be over me getting high."

"Hmm," Nick hummed, nodding his head. "Wanna fuck?"

"Right now, or in general?"

"In general," Nick said, as if he'd come to the conclusion that it should happen seconds before.

"No," Blake chuckled. "I don't want to fuck."

"I've never gotten down with a dude. I should probably see if I like it."

"Yeah, well, you're going to have to find another guy. You're not my type."

"You're not mine either," Nick shrugged. "Hey, what's wrong with me?"

"Specifically, or like, on a grand scale?"

"Why am I not your type?"

"You're just not," Blake replied, rolling his eyes at Nick's grimace. "Don't get butt-hurt about it. You said I wasn't yours either."

"That's because you're not a chick. I can appreciate what you have going on though," Nick stated, waving his hand in Blake's general direction. "I don't even know if I'd really be into it, but I'm pressed that you don't want to fuck me."

"I'm sure you'll get over it," Blake said easily. "Come in," he called when he heard his mother's gentle rap on the door. "You're home early," he noted as Grace entered the room.

"Why's the window open?" she asked skeptically. "It's freezing out there."

"Nick gets anxiety and sometimes he needs some fresh air," Blake explained, watching as his mother narrowed her blue eyes at him.

"I'm really weird," Nick nodded. "That's one of my many quirks."

"Okay," Grace said slowly, still eyeing Blake down. "I picked up your prescriptions this morning," she continued, putting them on top of his dresser.

"Thanks."

"I want you to stick around for dinner, Blake. I have a surprise for you," his mom stated. "You're more than welcome to stay, Nick. We're having meatloaf. Nothing fancy."

"I'm the opposite of fancy," Nick assured. "If fancy is over here," he held up a hand, "I'm way over here," and with that, he practically threw himself across the bed.

"So dramatic," Blake giggled, clearing his throat when he realized he had, in fact, giggled. Maybe he was higher than he thought.

"I don't know what kind of funny business you two are up to, but I know you're up to something," Grace asserted. "You better not be doing drugs." She scanned the room with work-tired eyes.

"The only drugs in here are the ones you just brought in," Blake lied, pointing to the prescription bags.

"Alright," Grace uttered, giving Blake one last suspicious glance before closing the door behind her.

"Smooth," Nick remarked, pulling the pipe out from under Blake's pillow.

"Put it in your backpack, alright," Blake directed. "We'll finish off my bag when we get out of here." He scoffed at Nick's unimpressed expression as he crossed the room to stow away his bowl. "You're getting dinner out of the deal. Don't complain."

"Is your mom a good cook?" Nick asked, walking over to Blake's dresser.

"She's decent," Blake replied, watching as his friend picked up his prescriptions and looked over the label. "Don't touch my shit, Holgate."

"Vin and Adderall," Nick read, pursing his lips. "Nice. Do you have ADD?"

"ADHD."

"Did you know Adderall can give you an awesome high?"

Blake crinkled his nose. "I take it every day and it's never gotten me high."

"You're taking it wrong," Nick replied, lifting his eyebrows mischievously. "Want me to show you?"

"Show me what?"

"You have to crush it, cut it like coke, and bump the lines," Nick informed, "and enjoy the high. Let's do it."

"I'm not snorting my medication, douchebag."

"I'll snort it for you."

Blake shook his head at the suggestion. "You're not snorting my meds either."

"You're no fun."

"You know damn well that's not true. I'm fun as fuck," Blake said, chucking a pillow at Nick.

"But on Adderall you'd be even more fun. Believe me, you'd feel like a star, shining bright and hot as hell, sparkling for all the world to see."

"That sounds like a messed-up Christmas carol."

"You'd be the angel on top of the tree," Nick continued, throwing the pillow back at Blake before tossing himself onto the bed. "A spiritual experience."

"You're selling this stuff hard."

"I just want a hit," Nick confessed.

"No shit," Blake chuckled. "You're not subtle."

"If you ever decide to take the leap, I hope you'll think of me."

"Think of you while I'm getting high or invite you over to partake?" Blake teased.

"You don't want to fuck me so just call me to come over and snort the shit, dick," Nick laughed.

"Don't hold your breath."

While Blake was enthusiastic about his alcohol and weed consumption, the idea of moving into anything harder wasn't appealing to him. Being fucked up was awesome and helped him deal with the shit he'd been going through, but he could stop smoking and drinking whenever he wanted to. Playing around with a substance that had the ability to make him a fiend wasn't a path he wanted to take. There were, of course, people who could mess with coke and the like and not get hooked, but Blake didn't know if he was that type of person.

"Dinner!" Grace called, interrupting the conversation about video games Blake and Nick had fallen into.

Nick smacked his lips eagerly as they sat down at the kitchen table. "I'm ready to grub on some meatloaf, Ms. Mitchell. Thanks for the invite."

"We never eat dinner together," Logan noted. "You're not going to tell us you're pregnant or something, are you?"

"Bite your tongue," Grace chided, cringing at the question. "Actually, before we get started, let's go outside."

"It's cold out," Blake reminded her.

"This will only take a minute," she promised.

"Dom's not out there waiting to do some corny proposal is he?" Blake asked, the prospect causing him to shudder.

"No. C'mon," Grace said waving them up.

"Your kids are annoying," Dominic stated as he followed on Blake's heels.

"I'll keep them around anyway," Grace grinned, ruffling Blake's hair.

"What's that?" Logan questioned, standing in the porch and pointing at a blue Saturn parked in the driveway.

"That's your Christmas present," she replied proudly. "Well, both of yours. You'll share it."

Blake's jaw dropped. A car. Their mom bought them a car. "How did you afford this?" he asked, knowing that as usual, money was tight.

"Dominic knew a guy. I got it for a very reasonable price. Don't worry."

"Badass. You have wheels!" Nick exclaimed, and Blake knew he was thinking of all the parties the ride could get them, too.

"It'll be a while before Blake will drive it," Logan said, jogging down the steps so he could get a closer look at the car. "No license means it's mine for a while."

"Maybe this will inspire Blake to get his permit," Grace reasoned, grinning at Blake. "Give you some extra inspiration."

"I'm inspired," Blake confirmed. He didn't know why he'd been dragging his feet on taking the permit test, but the promise of having a car to drive when he got it definitely lit a fire under his ass. Having a car would mean more freedom, something Blake constantly craved. "Thanks, Mom," he said, hugging her before joining Logan inside the car.

"It feels good," Logan called out the window to Grace. "Thank you."

"My pleasure," she said, approaching the driver's side of the car to hand Logan the keys. "You should take it for a quick spin."

"I'm in," Blake affirmed, smiling at his brother. "Gun it."

"This isn't the type of car that you 'gun.'" Logan laughed.

"It could be," Nick stated. "People will drag race anything. You guys could drive it a few miles and find tons of ready participants.

"But you'll do no such thing," Grace reminded. "I didn't get you this car so that you could wreck it on day one, and Heaven forbid you two get hurt...Take it for a quick spin and come back while your dinner's still hot."

"You got it, Mom," Logan said, unlocking the back door that Nick was attempting to open. "We'll be back in a couple of minutes."

Blake buckled his seatbelt as his brother backed out of the driveway. Although it would be a while before he could legally drive it, Blake knew it wouldn't be long before he took the old girl for a whirl. He couldn't wait to feel the steering wheel under his hands, empowered by the fact that he had control of where it turned.

10

It had taken approximately one week from Nick's mention of snorting Adderall for Blake to give it a try. He didn't call Nick like he requested. He didn't want anyone to know what he was doing. He knew Nick would be in and think it was great that he had begun taking his medication up his nose, but Blake knew better. It wasn't something he was proud of, but damn if he didn't enjoy having his head in the clouds. Things that would have bothered him sober couldn't reach him when he was high. The start of the second semester was pain-free as the chemicals snapped and sizzled through his veins, charging his body with confidence, lighting him up. Suddenly he was above everything—his classmates, his worries, his insecurities. He was the sun, too hot to be touched, a ball of fire unconcerned about the land he could leave scorched beneath him when he lacked a filter. But he kept burning, be it through his Adderall prescription, which kept a steady succession of creamsicle powder packed in his nose after school, or the joints he rolled with Greg. The best way to ease himself down.

The late nights should have affected Blake's academics, but it seemed they were destined to remain untouched by his inebriated existence. He couldn't help but wonder if he would have struggled had he stayed in private school or if he was smart enough to have gotten away with doing his homework fucked up there, too. The drugs told him he was, that he could have done well anywhere— boarding school, the University of Kentucky, fucking Harvard. He was a goddamn scholar ready to get his PhD in life, summa cum laude. He'd figured out how to make everything better.

It was rudimentary, and at seventeen he was already the valedictorian. Greg and Ian didn't get it. They were increasingly worried about Blake's drug use, but Blake was pretty sure that was because they weren't messing with Adderall. His friends were used to marijuana and its kicked back qualities, the natural shit that was nothing like the synthetic speed he was taking in. He was beyond just being alive. He was on a different plane, and that was okay. He didn't need anyone to co-sign his shit, but if he did, Nick would've been an eager partner. Nick understood what it was like to breathe rare air. When it came down to it, Blake wasn't like Nick. Nick was destined for prison. There was no doubt in Blake's mind that his friend wouldn't make it a few months past his eighteenth birthday without doing time. At seventeen, Nick had already done several stints in juvie on charges that would have gotten him harsher sentences as an adult. Unlike Logan, who had promptly cleaned up his act after being tossed into a juvenile correctional facility, Nick never changed. Sometimes, Blake wondered if Nick knew what a lost cause he was, but he never perseverated on it because he didn't want to lose the company. People got sensitive when you told them they had a problem, and Nick's issues made him an easy companion.

Shit wasn't easy with anyone else, though. In addition to the concern Greg had been showing for months, Grace and Logan were becoming more tuned in to Blake's extracurricular activities. They weren't aware of what exactly he was doing, but they knew something had changed. During hours of sobriety, Blake regretted the fact that they worried about him, that they struggled to understand his pain and that he was too weak to tell them. There was no strength in avoidance, he knew that, but it didn't mean he was ready to face things head on. He'd been doing a great job of avoiding just about everything that mattered to him, save the drugs.

When he entered his second semester military history class and found that both Claire and Xander were in it, he'd barely batted an eyelash. It was easier to cope with everything when he knew a magic powder would sort it out. He hated how reliant he was on the escape but loved the opportunity to float away.

Blake wasn't ignorant enough not to realize that he was in a precarious place. He should have been able to feel happy without lines of Adderall lifting his mood. In theory, he knew that. It was difficult seeing beyond the immediate outcome, the instant gratification that promised he was more content than genuine. He always thought he existed in the gray areas—not happy and not sad, not gay and not straight—so, living somewhere in the middle of his baseline in an Adderall induced euphoria was surprisingly tolerable, though he much preferred the higher plane.

"Do you want me to state the obvious?" Greg asked as he and Blake sat at their usual table in the cafeteria.

"Anyone who says 'yeah, sure,' to a question like that is a glutton for punishment."

"You would know about being a glutton for punishment, wouldn't you?" Greg challenged.

"Subtlety is out the window, huh?" Blake mused.

"The time for subtlety has passed."

"Well, I get the implication," Blake promised. "And I don't disagree."

"And yet...no change. You're still out there partying on school nights, checked out mentally, going downhill quick, man."

Blake sighed. He could only imagine the shit Greg would give him if he actually knew what Blake was up to. He wasn't running to tell anyone about his new habit, certainly not Greg and not Nick either. Blake didn't take pride in the fact that he was snorting his medication. He didn't think it was cool or respectable, but he did think it was a perfect escape, like exhaling a breath he'd been holding in for too long. Maybe if he were fucking around with the drug socially he wouldn't have felt as much shame. There was something tawdry about the level of secrecy. Blake found, however, that the best remedy for the dark feelings was more Adderall.

"I think you chill with Nick too often," Greg continued, taking a bite of his soft pretzel.

"Jealous?" Blake asked, raising an eyebrow.

"That's beside the point," Greg replied. "The guy's a textbook bad influence, the perpetual devil on your shoulder."

"And let me guess, you're the angel?"

"Fuck no," Greg laughed. "I'd crush those well-sculpted shoulders sitting up there."

Blake chuckled, shaking his head at Greg's penchant for self-deprecation. "Listen, I get that you're worried about me and I understand why, okay? But shit isn't as bad as you're making it out to be. I'm fine. Everybody's allowed to let loose once in a while, right?"

"One in a while," Ian scoffed.

"Where the fuck did you come from?" Blake chided his constantly distracted friend.

"I've been sitting here listening to you yammer for the last twenty minutes," Ian replied.

"I think that was a rhetorical question. Man, you're such a cute kid," Greg sighed, leaning across the table to pat Ian's freckled cheek.

"Fuck off," Ian laughed, shooing Greg's hand away.

"I hate to cut this short," Blake began as he stood up and pushed his chair in, "but I don't want to hang out with you guys anymore."

"That's nice," Greg tsked, giving Blake the finger.

"It's not me it's you," he smirked, tousling his friend's blond mop. "I'll see you later."

With that, Blake exited the cafeteria and walked toward the field. Settling into his usual spot under the bleachers, he lit a cigarette and closed his eyes as he took the first drag. The more attention people paid him, the more he wished they'd ignore him. It wasn't like he didn't enjoy the spotlight, he did, but only when it was for all the right reasons and not his current disposition.

He was nonplussed by the sound of the bell ringing, intent on finishing his smoke before heading to class. By the time he showed up to Military History, he was fifteen minutes late and Mr. Porter was not impressed.

"You're late, Blake," the teacher admonished as Blake slid into his seat.

"Looks to be that way," Blake agreed, glancing at the clock.

"And you came with sass," Mr. Porter noted, typing something into his laptop.

"It happens," Blake nodded.

While it was rare for Blake to talk back to teachers, or any other authority figure, he was sick of everyone being on his ass about everything. Nobody was giving him space to breathe.

"So does detention, and I'm giving you four days of it. Let's do two for tardiness and two for insubordination," Mr. Porter decided.

Blake could feel all eyes on him, yet he refused to give them any reaction. He did, however, look to his left to catch Claire's. She appeared to be more concerned than confused. He hated the notes of sympathy on her face, the hint of pity.

"Four days," Blake repeated, as if he had to somehow agree to the sentence.

"Why don't we try to avoid making it five?" Mr. Porter warned, clearly not interested in dealing with Blake's newfound attitude.

Deciding that he'd also had enough for the day, Blake kept his mouth shut for the rest of the class, zoning out of the lecture as he thought about what kind of trouble he could get himself into later that night. He knew he should stay home and study for his permit so he could finally—legally—drive the car his mother had bought him months before, but he was more interested in getting wasted.

Sneaking his phone onto his lap, he opened his conversation with Nick.

Blake (1:32pm): What are we doing tonight?
Nick (1:33pm): Is the correct answer getting messed up?
Blake (1:33pm): Sounds about right.
Nick (1:34pm): Well then that's what we're doing.
Blake (1:34pm): I can always count on you.

Nick (1:35pm): It's like I'm the king of fucked up things.
Blake (1:35pm): All hail King Dick.
Nick (1:36pm): Was that autocorrect?
Blake (1:36pm): Nope.
Nick (1:37pm): Didn't think so.
Nick (1:37pm): Savage.
Blake (1:38pm): That's me.
At least today.

Blake knew he should have called it a night after round one of the revelry, but he was too chock full of adrenaline and Adderall to settle down. The University of Kentucky basketball team had won the championship, and it was epic. He didn't want to miss a moment of the celebration. The prior months had been a blur of drugs, detentions, and stress, so it was easy for Blake to rationalize that he deserved some pure, unadulterated elation.

Since he was home in time for curfew, his mother had gone to sleep, which gave him the perfect opportunity to sneak out to continue partying. There was a moment, as Blake stared up at the ceiling before climbing out of the bed to put on his hoodie, that he considered not going, thought about being moderately responsible, but he figured there was no point in starting then. Especially when Kentucky was alive with UK pride.

Bending down to tie his shoes, Blake held his breath, trying to hear beyond the door to make certain his mom and Logan had turned in. The singular sound of the soft whirl from the vents assured him that the coast was clear. As gingerly as possible, Blake turned the knob on his door and pushed it open slowly, grimacing when the hinges squeaked. Already committed to the feat, Blake began to creep down the hallway, strategically avoiding the floorboards he knew would creak if he put pressure on them. One misstep and his intention to leave the house would be loudly announced. Carefully, he descended the stairwell on the tips of his toes, cringing with every step. When he reached level ground, he picked up his pace, grabbing the keys to the car from the bowl on the foyer table.

As soon as Blake exited the house, he let out a relieved sigh, standing still for a moment to savor the cool, early-April air. He made it. Deciding it was best to manually open the door, he slid into the driver's seat and shifted the gear to neutral. Instead of starting the car, he got out and pushed it to the street, only putting the key in the ignition when it was far enough down the road that if his mother did hear it, she'd think it was the neighbor's.

His lack of a license should have been in the forefront of his mind, but it was nothing more than a fleeting thought as he drove toward Nick's house.

Blake (1:22am): I'll be there in 10. Come outside.

Nick (1:23am): You have the car?!

Blake (1:23am): Yup.

Nick (1:24am): Fucking badass

Nick (1:24am): I got the party lined up

Blake (1:25am): You better.

Nick (1:25am): Just said I did. Pay attention to driving.

Blake tossed his phone onto the passenger seat, focusing on the winding, country road. He'd sobered up enough from the first party to know he was fine, but he couldn't deny that he had a case of tired eyes. He knew how to perk himself up, but he'd wait until he got to the party.

Nick always had the hookup. For a guy who didn't seem to have many friends, he had a ton of people to get wasted with, and those people were privy to where everyone was partying. Though it was nearly two in the morning, the stranger's house they were standing in was packed with loud, drunk teenagers. Blake wondered who the "host" was and where the hell their parents were. He wasn't complaining, but it floored him that other teens had so much access and freedom.

"Beer bong," Nick said, elbowing Blake to draw his eyes away from the attractive guy toking across the room. He had sleeves of tattoos and a perfect mouth, attributes that intrigued Blake enough that he promised himself he'd go talk to him after he got more shitty.

Tilting his head, he placed the hose in his mouth, swallowing quickly as a deluge of warm Natty Light poured down his throat. Once he'd taken it all in, Blake stood up straight and wiped his mouth with the back of his hand.

"Pretty good form, Mitchell," Nick grinned, patting Blake's bicep. "But watch how an expert handles it."

Of all the things Blake could become an aficionado at, he was sure ingesting beer was at the bottom of his list, but he indulged his friend, who in all honesty, didn't have much more to strive toward.

Blake glanced at the hot tattooed guy again. He was decked out in red, from the Reds flat bill on his head, to the Jordans on his feet. Though it was an unconventional look for a white kid in Kentucky, Blake liked it. He probably would've approved of anything the guy was wearing, considering how good-looking he was. When their eyes locked, the guy held up the pipe as if offering to share, and Blake wasted no time in heading over to join him.

"I saw you looking over here. I figured you wanted to hit it," he smirked, handing the bowl over to Blake.

"You have no idea," Blake replied, returning the grin.

After his third drag, Blake was following the guy to the dark corner of a bedroom crowded with kids from another school who he didn't recognize. They snuck touches, turned on by the potential danger of being caught. Groping led to kissing, which somehow segued into Blake pulling a baggie of crushed Adderall out of his back pocket to share with his new friend. He'd never snorted the stuff socially, but in his already smashed state, he didn't give a damn.

The drugs managed to make Blake hornier than he had already been, which was a feat on its own.

"We should get outta here," the guy whispered against Blake's lips. "Do you have a car?"

"Yeah, but where could we go?" Blake asked. "Just park somewhere?"

"We could," he said, "or we could go back to my place. My dad's an alcoholic. He passed out for the night before I left, and he'll be out cold until at least noon tomorrow."

"Where do you live?"

"Millville."

Blake nodded. The town was a few miles past Unionville, but that worked out fine because he would be able to drop Nick off before he and the tattooed kid continued their fun. "Let's go."

They made their way into the living room where Blake located Nick, who appeared to be rounding the corner to the stupor stage of inebriation.

"We're leaving," Blake stated, nudging Nick's knee with his own. "Get up."

"Where are we going?" Nick slurred, standing up on visibly shaky legs.

"You're going home," Blake answered.

"Who're you?" Nick asked the tattooed guy.

Blake tuned in to hear the guy say, "Trent."

Trent.

"You're coming with us?" Nick asked, confused.

"Yeah," Trent nodded, smiling at Blake.

"Oh!" Nick exclaimed as if the switch to his brain had been flicked up. "Ohh."

Blake closed his eyes and shook his head, continuously astounded by how obtuse his friend could be.

"Well, then, lead the way," Nick said, gesturing for them to head out. "Shotgun."

"Are you good to drive?" Trent asked as he climbed in the back of the car and settled into the seat behind the passenger's.

"He's always good to drive," Nick interjected, buckling his seatbelt. "He's the best non-licensed driver on the road."

"That's reassuring," Trent chuckled.

"I'm alright," Blake promised, smiling back at him in the rearview mirror. That was probably a lie—what with the beer, weed, and Adderall—but he knew that on the continuum of being messed up, he'd been worse. It wasn't as if he was falling over or puking. That had to count for something.

"So, did your license get taken away or something?" Trent asked as Blake concentrated on the dark two-lane road. "DUI or whatever?"

"No, nothing like that," Blake answered. "I just haven't gotten it yet. Haven't gotten around to it, I guess."

"It's better to not have it than to lose it," Trent reasoned. "At least you still have a chance. I can't apply for one again until I'm twenty-one."

"No shit," Blake sighed. "What did they get you on?"

"Hotboxing."

"Stupid," Nick laughed.

Blake rolled his eyes and scoffed at his friend. "Like you wouldn't if you had a car."

"Well, it turns out I'm currently in a car and—" he finagled a pipe and lighter out of his pocket, "I have weed. Opportunity is knocking. Let's see if you're right, if I'll actually do it."

"Let's not, because I never doubted it," Blake retorted. His eyes were bleary and the last thing he needed was to have a cloud of smoke to contend with.

"No fun," Nick tsked, turning back to regard Trent. "What do you think?"

"I think I'm not driving so I'm gonna shut the fuck up," Trent replied, garnering a grin from Blake.

Trent was cool, more so than anyone he'd met recently, and Blake couldn't have been more excited to get to know him better. As he drove, he thought of how the rest of the night was going to go, hoping the fire they'd found at the party would continue to burn when it was just the two of them.

They were nearly to Unionville when Blake let out a yawn that assured him it was good they were close to their destination. All of a sudden, his hope for chemistry with Trent was a wish that he wouldn't fall asleep as soon as he hit the guy's bed. He was revving to go earlier, but now he thought he'd much rather go to sleep, as a wave of wooziness and fatigue washed over him.

The headlights of a passing truck blinded Blake for a moment, leaving floating, black blotches in his vision long after the vehicle was out of sight. Squeezing his eyes shut, Blake felt his body being tossed to the right and then to the left as everything grew quiet, vacuous, like the air was sucked out of the car completely. He was spinning in a clothes dryer, hot and discombobulated, head smacking the side with each revolution.

And then came the crash.

12

Blake wasn't sure he'd passed out until he came to with a skull-splitting headache and aching neck. In front of him was the thick trunk of a tree, slightly cracked by the now smashed hood of his car. Turning slowly to his left, he saw that he'd ended up in an embankment surrounded by sod and rocks. He wondered how it happened, one moment he was squinting and the next he could barely open his eyes.

"Fuck," he grunted.

"We got in an accident. You took the curve too quickly," Trent said from back, "We spun out. It's bad, man."

It wasn't as though Blake hadn't realized he'd crashed the car, it was more that he struggled to understand if it had really happened or if he was sleeping and existing within a nightmare. Trent's voice made it real, and his words had Blake snapping his head around to check on Nick.

"Holy shit!" Blake cried, staring at his friend's lifeless body. Nick was folded in on himself, head hanging low and shoulders rolled forward, with shards of glass covering his lap. "He's dead! What the fuck? He's dead!"

Reaching over, Blake pressed his fingers against the dip of Nick's neck, trying to find his pulse, praying that he would.

"I don't know—" Blake began, shaking his head vehemently in disbelief from what had occurred. He couldn't feel his friend's heartbeat. "I don't know if I'm doing this right or if he's dead. I don't know." All he knew was that he was panicking. Nick was dead, the car was totaled, and it was his fault.

"Get the fuck off me," Nick grumbled, knocking Blake's hand away. "I'm not dead."

"You looked dead," Blake said tentatively. He could hear the way his voice was warbling and wavering with anxiety. "I could've sworn you were dead."

"Well consider this the second second-coming," Nick snarked, pressing the heels of his hands against his eye-sockets. "You fucked your car up."

"You're not dead," Blake uttered, still flabbergasted by the development. "I thought you were done."

"Got it," Nick nodded, pushing on the airbag that was encroaching on his space. "I'm not though."

"He's in shock," Trent stated.

Blake wanted to disagree, to repeat that he really believed Nick was dead, but he didn't, because maybe Trent was right. He was sitting in the car he'd stolen and then crashed into a ditch, in the middle of the night, and he was probably in shock.

"I can't get out," Nick groused, attempting to unlock the door and push it open. "Try yours."

Blake did as he was told, relieved for the directions that helped him function in his state. "I can't either."

The sound of a tired power window inching down drew Blake's attention to the backseat where he saw Trent's face was full of blood.

"Jesus Christ, you're bleeding; your face is covered in blood," Blake stammered, unable to see Trent's expression clearly beyond the crimson splatter.

"It's my nose," Trent informed, using his already blood-soaked red t-shirt to wipe the substance off his skin. "It's broken."

"Shit," Blake whispered. "I'm sorry."

"Whatever," Trent said easily, "it's not the first time and probably won't be the last." He gestured to the open window. "We can get out this way. Are you hurt or anything? Can you do that?"

"I don't think I'm hurt," Blake replied, unbuckling his seatbelt. "You go first."

Blake watched as Trent maneuvered his lithe body out of the window. He hit the ground with a thud, and called, "I'm okay."

"Roll over or I'm going to land on you," Nick ordered as he made his way through the window. "Come on, Mitchell."

The act of climbing out of a car window would have typically been easy for Blake, but he found it difficult to focus on the task at hand. After a bit of a struggle, he was lying in the cool soil, staring up at the pitch-black sky, wishing what happened hadn't. Silently, he compelled the universe to reverse time.

"Shit," Nick sighed, assessing the car's damage. "It's fucking wrecked."

Sitting up so he no longer had to peer at his friend through his peripheral vision, Blake took his first look at the vehicle, awed by the level of destruction. His mom was going to kill him, and then after she did, his brother would end him again. He had no business driving the car to begin with, and there was no doubt they would both remind him of that, exponentially.

"We have to leave it here," Blake decided. "They'll think it was stolen or something and the person wrecked it."

"I mean, technically that's the truth," Nick said, "but, I think they'll know it was your dumbass who did it."

Blake shook his head. "No, I'll sneak back into the house before they wake up, get in bed, and when they notice it's gone I'll act shocked."

"I don't know anything about anything, but I don't think that's going to work," Trent interjected.

"It's not like I have a lot of fucking options here," Blake snapped, rubbing the back of his neck to calm himself down. "Do you guys have anyone we can call to pick us up?"

"At three thirty?" Nick scoffed. "Yeah, right."

"You know a shit ton of people," Blake exclaimed. "You don't know one that would come get us?"

"I know partiers," he replied, "not the kinda guys who are gonna do me a solid in the middle of the night."

"I guess we're walking then," Blake sighed. A four-mile trek was the last thing he wanted to do, but he knew there weren't any other options.

As they started their journey, Blake half-wondered where Trent was going to go, but he mostly didn't care. He had enough on his mind. With every step he took, he dreaded the next, knowing he was drawing closer to the inevitable at home, while moving further from the car and the responsibilities he'd abandoned in the embankment.

It was nearly four thirty by the time he unlocked the front door to his house. Blake had expected everyone to be sound asleep, and was unpleasantly surprised to find his mother, brother and Dominic sitting in the living room, watching him as he crept in.

"Where were you?" Grace demanded, her jaw clenched as she glared at him. His mother had made it clear that she was sick and tired of his poor behavior, and Blake had no doubt that his antics that evening would push her over the edge.

"Out," he answered vaguely. There was no good answer to where he'd been and what he'd done.

"I got that much," she tsked. "Where were you? Where are your glasses?"

Blake brought his hand to his face, surprised to find his specs weren't on. He thought things were blurry, but he was in too much of a haze to realize why.

"Where's my car?" Logan interrupted, arms crossed over his chest.

"Our car," Blake corrected, earning sighs and head shakes from everyone, including Dominic, which was a fucking joke.

"You don't have a license. Until you do, it's mine," Logan shot back. "Where's *my* car?"

"In a ditch somewhere," Blake admitted, barely able to croak out the words. "I got into an accident."

"You have to be fucking kidding me!" Logan growled, looking like a tiger about to lunge at his prey.

"Are you hurt?" Grace cried, her "mom-reflex" flexing as she jumped up from the couch to examine him.

"He's about to be," Logan grunted, pacing the room and punching his fist against his thigh. Blake would've told him to calm down if he'd been able to muster the balls.

"Uh, no," Blake mumbled, hating that he'd caused his mom to worry when she already had so much on her plate.

"I can't believe you," she growled, shaking her head in disgust. If he didn't have whiplash from the wreck, he surely had it from the rapid change in his mother's disposition. "When does it end with you? When is enough, enough?"

"I don't know how to answer that," Blake whispered, avoiding eye contact with his mother. When he risked a glance, he saw that her water lines were pooling with tears. She'd survived cancer, and now she had to survive him.

"Well maybe you should think about it," Dominic suggested.

If Blake hadn't been so exhausted he would've told Dom off for being a hypocrite. Instead, he listened to his mother and Logan go off about all the things he needed to do at daybreak while he tried not to pass out. By the time he did tuck himself into bed, he made a mental note never to leave again.

That worked well for approximately an hour, until his mother was banging on his bedroom door, ordering him to get up so they could go look for the car. Because of how grueling the walk home had been, Blake had thought the car was further outside of Unionville than it actually was.

While they assessed the damage, Grace chanted a medley of "I can't believe this" and "what the hell, Blake," while Blake searched the wreckage for his glasses, a task that would have been much easier if he had his glasses on. When he did locate his frames, he was happy to see they weren't broken, but disappointed to find that the lenses had popped out. Running his hand over the patchy grass in the general vicinity of where he'd found his glasses, he came across the lenses—unscratched.

Blake finagled the lenses back into the frames thinking how, sometimes, he was too lucky for his own good.

13

T he months following the accident were full of contrition. Blake knew he'd lost his mother's trust, and regardless of how uphill the battle was, he wanted to make shit right as best he could. Seeing as how he couldn't afford to replace the car, or turn back time, Blake decided that his best course of action moving forward was to clean up his act. So, he did. Rather than spend the majority of his time with Nick, he was back to party-free weekdays and afternoons with Greg, who thankfully forgave him for his attitude and didn't say "I told you so," even though he probably wanted to.

To make matters more interesting, Blake had managed to reconnect with Claire in some capacity. They weren't exactly heading quickly toward coupledom, but they were talking, and Blake was back to working on his "master plan." So far, the plan consisted of walking her to her locker after class each day while stealing glances and touches that he knew turned her on. She wasn't putty in his hands, but she was softening, which was progress.

"What are you doing after school today?" Blake asked on their daily post-military history walk.

"Studying," she replied, hugging her notebook to her chest. "Just like you should be."

"I'm planning on studying," he smirked, adding, "with you."

"Oh, is that right?" Claire laughed.

Blake loved how she threw her head back when she giggled at his jokes, as if he was worthy of more than just the noise.

"Is it?" he asked, raising an eyebrow. "It sounds like fun, doesn't it? Hitting the books for old times' sake."

"Are you pretending that we studied?" Claire questioned, with a grin. "I tried to study, and you tried to make-out."

"You never complained."

"Never," she confirmed, her cheeks flushing at the admission.

"So, do you want to?" Blake pressed.

"Want to what?"

He smiled the smile he knew drove her crazy. "Study with me."

Claire looked around the hallway as if an answer was written somewhere on the walls. "Okay," she said, her eyes finally locked on Blake's. "We can study."

Unsure if Claire had agreed to a study or a make-out session, Blake nodded, feeling pretty good about either. Progress.

"Where should we go?" she asked, adjusting the backpack straps on her shoulders. "The library?"

She must have been playing it coy. There was no way she didn't know what he was going to suggest, but he gave her the courtesy of letting her have her game. "How about my house, Claire?"

Biting her lip, she considered the proposal before nodding her head. "Alright."

As they walked down the hallway and out of the school, Blake reminded himself that she had a boyfriend, that there was no chance she would actually let herself go enough to be with him, even for an afternoon.

"Marni's been asking about you," she said as they ambled onto the sidewalk to Blake's house. They'd made the trek many times before, but it had been so long since they'd been together like this.

Fluffy white clouds passed overhead as the late-May sun warmed their faces. If it hadn't been spring, being next to Claire would have made it feel like it was. Blake wanted to grasp for her hand, interlace their fingers, hold her as they walked, but he refrained, worried the show of affection would scare her away.

"I haven't talked to her in a while," Blake noted. Even the mention of his friend's name was a blast from the still not so distant past. "How's she doing?"

"Well," Claire replied. "She was in Lexington for a while but now she's back in Unionville. You should text her. She'd love to hear from you."

"We should all hang out," Blake suggested, earning him an eye-roll from Claire. "What?"

"We aren't even past this study session and you're already planning ahead."

"Master planning," Blake corrected with a wink.

"You just winked."

"I did."

She laughed. "Who winks?"

"I guess me sometimes," he laughed. "There's a lot going on here."

"So much," Claire agreed, bumping into Blake with her shoulder playfully.

Though Blake was glad his mom was at work, he almost wished she would have been home when he led Claire through the front door. Grace loved Claire. There wasn't much not to adore. As far as Grace was concerned, Claire was a pillar of responsibility and good Christian values. It wouldn't be bad if his mother thought even an iota of that goodness could rub off on him.

Fuck, Blake wanted to rub up on Claire.

"Where are the cats?" she asked, wrapping her fingers around the straps of her bag, a security blanket.

"Probably upstairs," he answered. "Do you want to go look for them?"

"Okay." She nodded and followed Blake up the stairs. It was hard to believe that Claire was in his house to begin with, and the fact that she was now climbing the steps to his room was otherwise unfathomable. He thought about this moment so many times since she dumped him, but never thought it would become a reality. Good shit didn't happen in his life anymore. His streak of bad luck—and choices—had convinced him of that.

"Hey cutie. Where's your brother?" Claire cooed, dropping to her knees so she could pet Chewy, a cat who was generally cranky toward anyone but her. It was unbelievable that even after a year, the cat remained warm toward her.

"You're going to give him a big head with all that affection," Blake chuckled.

Claire pursed her lips. "That sounds like the same reservations I have with giving you attention," she teased.

"Believe me, my head's not big, especially not after the last few months. Someone who fucks up as much as me can't be cocky."

"That's not true. Maybe it's your cockiness that keeps you messing up. It convinces you that you won't get caught or get in any trouble."

"Are you taking psychology this year?" he questioned, worried that she'd somehow developed the ability to read him like a book.

Claire shook her head, standing up straight. "No, but you're easy."

"You're not," Blake promised her, as if she didn't already know.

"That's true," she conceded, smiling as he moved closer to her.

Blake had to take the chance. There wouldn't be many others. Claire was in a relationship, but she was also in his room, right in front of him, looking beautiful and open. He would be stupid not to try something, anything, to connect with her again. Sliding his hands into the small gaps between Claire's shoulders and the straps, Blake pushed the bag off her back while simultaneously leaning down to slot his lips against hers. She reciprocated, wrapping her arms around his neck as he deepened the kiss. Placing his hands on her hips, he pulled her in closer, relieved she didn't resist.

Their kisses grew more feverish as they stripped off their clothes, a culmination of months of anticipation and want. Falling onto the bed, Blake attempted to kick his pants off his ankles, yanking them off when they ended up tangled. He grinned as Claire kissed his neck, her hands traveling over his body. Wrapping his arms around her waist, he flipped her over, so he was leaning on top of her. Blake placed a hand tenderly on her cheek, gazing into her eyes.

"Is this alright?" he asked, aware that her body was as ready as his, but worried her mind might not be.

"I'm still a virgin," she whispered, the statement causing Blake an immense amount of relief. He was glad she didn't give it up to what's-his-name. Maybe there was hope for Blake yet.

"We don't have to—" he began, sitting up, only to be yanked down by Claire.

"I want to," Claire promised with a sexy little smile.

"Yeah?" Blake asked, hearing the excitement in his own voice.

She nodded. "Yeah."

Blake scrambled off the bed to get a condom out of the shoebox in his closet and hurried back to Claire. It was hard to believe it was about to happen. He'd thought about the moment for so long and, finally, his fantasies about Claire were about to become a reality. While he'd had plenty of sex in the past, being with Claire felt different, special in a lot of ways he hadn't expected.

As they lay in bed holding each other after they were done, Blake's mind spun, wondering how things would change between them. He hoped Claire would end things with her boyfriend and be with him, but he couldn't help but be tentative about the idea of getting back with her. Their breakup had been difficult, and as much as he liked Claire, he didn't want to go through that shit again.

Tucking a lock of hair behind her ear, Blake kissed her cheek. He wasn't sure things would pan out between them, but he wanted things to be okay, at least for a little while.

"That was nice," she said softly, grinning when his eyes went wide.

"Nice? A walk in the park is *nice*, a bouquet of flowers is *nice*. That was better than *nice*."

She giggled. "Hmm, let me think about how I'd describe it then..."

"How about Earth-shakingly awesome?" he suggested, tapping his fingers on his defined pecs. "I think that would be fair."

"Definitely fair," she agreed, "but I was going to say mind-blowingly amazing."

"I could settle for that," Blake grinned. "That sounds pretty good."

"It was pretty good."

He laughed. "No. That's a downgrade from mind-blowingly amazing."

Claire pressed her lips against his. "Then we'll stick with mind-blowingly amazing. I feel confident about that."

"You should feel confident about a lot of things," he flirted, pulling her in closer. "So many things."

"Is that right?" she hummed.

"That's right," he assured.

It was true.

PART II

SENIOR

14

Blake turned eighteen a week before his senior year, and while it was a milestone moment, he instantly felt a pressure he hadn't expected in regards to his new adult status. The dumb things he'd done the year before would have meant serious time if he'd been caught doing them at a legal age. He needed to be smarter, to make better decisions, keep his nose clean, and focus.

Summer was surprisingly wonderful. Though things were still strained with his mother and brother, Blake had made some headway in gaining their trust back simply by fucking up less. He consistently made it home before curfew and helped out around the house more than he had in the past. There was something to be said for being responsible. It alleviated the tinges of guilt he felt when he complicated shit for his mom.

Blake had spent the majority of the sunny, sweaty days with Greg, laughing and feeling more grounded than he had in a while. They got into typical teenage shenanigans, but everything was lighter with Greg than it was with Nick. Smoking weed in the dugouts of the high school baseball field felt like a rite of passage with Greg rather than an escape. Blake was present, something he hadn't wanted to be, but knew he should have been. His behavior was far from angelic, but it was further from devilish. There was no secret sniffing of prescription medication or driving under the influence of anything. Things felt pure and idyllic in comparison to how heavy they'd been during the school year.

Summer days spent with Claire had been more complicated than the ones Blake enjoyed with Greg. She'd broken up with her boyfriend shortly after she and Blake had slept together but made it clear to Blake that she planned to stay single. Ideally, he would have wanted to be with her, but the fact that they were still screwing from time to time was a good consolation. When it came down to it, though he desired more, things were simple, which was exactly what Blake needed. He had one more year of high school and he knew he'd benefit from an increased commitment to graduate.

The fantasy of getting out of Kentucky was more intoxicating than the Adderall had ever been. Attending boarding school in North Carolina in his freshman year had been good for him. Blake liked being in a new place, meeting new people, having a new life. It was appealing that he could have that again in college. Though he knew wrestling was off the table, his grades were exceptional, which would make getting in to at least a few universities a piece of cake.

Imagining himself in college was a guilty pleasure. Sometimes Blake would allow his mind to wander to what life would be like in a dorm full of other guys who were smart, hot and horny. No doubt there would be dudes who were too scared to come out in high school but were finally ready to explore a whole new world of dick. Blake would be happy to be their guide. He wondered if college kick-backs were different than the high school parties he frequented. They had to be better, everything had to be better when there was more freedom.

"Funny seeing you here," Greg grinned as he walked toward Blake, who was sitting on the curb outside WCHS.

"It's such a coincidence," Blake teased, taking his friend's outstretched hand and allowing Greg to yank him up. Flashes of the first day of junior year popped into Blake's mind, and it was night and day how different he felt. Although he'd begun eleventh grade with a sense of dread, the start of senior year felt hopeful and settled. He'd come a long way. He just had to keep on moving forward.

"How are you feeling?" Greg asked as they headed into the high school.

"Ready to get in and get this year done."

"It's not a good sign that you have senioritis on the first day, man."

Blake smirked. "I think I caught that shit sophomore year. Is 'sophomoritis' a thing?"

"You're a trailblazer. Emphasis on the 'blazer.'"

"Speaking of which, are we chilling after school?"

"I don't see why not. We're putting in time. I'd say we're earning a future brain break," Greg nodded. "At least it's something to look forward to."

"I like the way you think. Where's Ian at? He hasn't been around lately?" Blake asked. He wasn't as close with the redhead as he was to Greg, but he liked spending time with him here and there.

"He's with Kelsey now," Greg explained. "I think she's holding his balls in a vise. He holds her purse at the mall and stuff, brings her Starbucks. It's the new and improved Ian."

"He could do worse. It's not a bad thing he's busting his ass to make her happy."

"Not a bad thing at all," Greg agreed. "Plus, it makes me laugh."

"Which is always important," Blake chuckled.

"Tremendously."

As they walked past Jeremiah Burbar and a few other guys on the wrestling team, Blake was relieved that he didn't experience the waves of shame or surges of anger he'd felt the last time he was in their presence. He didn't forgive them for the fact that they were ignorant pieces of shit, but his rage had markedly subsided. Deep down, Blake wished he would have gone with his first instinct after the alienation and enrolled at a rival school, so he could hand them their asses on the mat. Circumstances had been too crazy to follow through on the fantasy, but that hadn't stopped Blake from daydreaming about it.

"You should join up again," Greg suggested once the idiots were out of earshot.

Blake stopped in his tracks to study his friend's face for an ounce of jest. He couldn't find it. "You're fucking serious?"

"Dead serious."

"Why would I ever do that after the way things went down last year?"

"Because you love wrestling," he stated matter-of-factly. "You're good at it and those guys don't have the right to keep you from doing something you love and are good at. That's why."

"You have to get these idealistic, triumphant scenarios out of your mind. You do it with everything and the only thing it's going to lead to is disappointment. Things don't always work out the way they should. Those are the facts."

"They're hardly facts. They're impressions from a jaded mind. That level of skepticism can't be trusted."

Blake shook his head and laughed. "You've gotten really philosophical in your old age."

"Senior year's looking good on me," Greg agreed. "But, in all honesty, you should go for it, get back out there, be the beast I know you are."

"Yeah," Blake cringed. "I think I'll pass on that."

"Their loss then, and yours, too."

"Debatable."

"You know I'm always willing to debate."

"Of course, it's one of your worst qualities," Blake retorted, patting his friend on the back.

"Speaking of bad qualities...Are you really dropping Lexington Tech this year?"

Blake raised an eyebrow in challenge. "How is that a bad thing? I didn't feel like I got much out of it last year, so I'm not wasting my time."

"Like you're not wasting your time with wrestling, yeah?" Greg pressed raising his eyebrows right back.

"You know what, how about we talk about you, G? We don't talk about you enough. How about I give you some shit for your bullshit?"

"Well, as fun as that sounds, the bell's about to ring," Greg replied with a mischievous grin.

"But it didn't ring yet," Blake pointed out. "I could get started..."

"The thing is, I'm a little more sensitive than you. Some may say, not as strong. You need a truth teller, I need a cheerleader, and I think you'd look amazing in a skirt. You have great legs and you're pretty limber."

"You're deflecting."

"Expertly," Greg agreed.

"It's not really expertly if I just called it out," Blake contended, hooking his new padlock on his locker and giving it a tug to make sure it was secure. "It's amateurish at best."

"We should share a locker, my homeroom is F12 and my locker's in B wing. Your locker is in a much better location for me."

"But walking is good for you, too. You said you wanted to shed a few pounds," Blake reminded, tickling his friend's belly.

"That was theoretical," Greg explained. "If the opportunity presented itself for me to lose some poundage in a miraculous way, I'd take it."

"I missed the miraculous caveat before."

"You have to pay better attention, Mitchell. I'm going to add that to my list," Greg teased, giving Blake a cheeky grin as the warning bell rang. "That's my cue to go."

"Pussy," Blake smirked, turning to make his way into his homeroom.

Unsurprisingly, Xander was already seated in one of the desks, but very surprisingly, Blake was unaffected by his presence. Last year the sight of the loudmouth filled Blake with anxiety, but the life he had lived since the first day of junior year had proven to him that there were worse things than the betrayal of a shitty human being and the negative reactions of equally crappy people. There was no weight in Xander being there, no omens of a bad year to come or self-fulfilling prophecies of failure.

Sliding into a desk in the front of the room, Blake waited for the announcements to begin, ready to get the day started and the year underway. Finally, there was light at the end of the scholastic drudgery tunnel and he was pretty sure it was the glow of his bright future.

15

———

Blake should have known shit was about to hit the fan. He'd made it until mid-October without a detention, and his life had been too idyllic for comfort. The cycle of turbulence that he'd had to contend with over the last several years never subsided long enough for Blake to believe he'd done the impossible and broken it. When things were going well for a significant period of time, Blake began to wonder when the other shoe was going to drop. It was hard to accept that perhaps he was on an upward trajectory, because if he did, he wouldn't be prepared when the positivity inevitably began to decline. It's why he wasn't surprised by the fact that a very trivial infraction at school had snowballed into a blizzard of bullshit.

As usual, Blake had left his nylon drawstring bag, which contained a baggie of weed, snacks and other miscellaneous crap in his stash spot outside the Circle K across the street from the high school. He wasn't dumb enough to risk bringing drugs into school, so he kept them in a divot behind a tree. That way, Blake didn't need to backtrack to his house after school before going to the park to get high with Greg and Ian. He'd been using the method for at least a year and never had a problem. It wasn't until he made the mistake of leaving his school issue iPad in the bag that his use of the stash spot blew up in his face.

"Mr. Mitchell," Ms. DelGracio called as Blake zoned out in English class. "Earth to Mr. Mitchell."

"Oh, sorry," Blake said, straightening up in his seat.

"Look around at your classmates," she continued, pointing in all directions as if Blake was unaware of where they were sitting. "What do they all have in common?"

"They're white?" Blake offered much to his teacher's chagrin.

"They all have their iPads out for editing," she stated. "I suggest you begin your assignment or you will have a good bit of homework to deal with tonight."

Leaning over to grab his iPad out the backpack he'd shoved under the chair, Blake sighed, realizing it wasn't there.

"Ms. DelGracio," he said, raising his hand. "I think it's in my locker. Can I have a pass to go get it?"

She shook her head. "Absolutely not. It's a privilege to have this technology and your irresponsibility won't be tolerated. Get out your silent reading book. You'll read for the remainder of the period and complete today's assignment tonight."

Thinking better than talking back, Blake bit his tongue and pulled *Brave New World* from his bag. He didn't mind having some extra work to do if it meant he could dive into the novel for a while. Blake was surprised by how much he enjoyed the dystopian classic, intrigued by Aldous Huxley's views on Fordism, economic balance, and societal values. It was the presence of the pill, *soma*, however, that stood out the most to him. At the sign of any unhappiness, all the characters had to do was pop a pill and it would dissipate. It was what he'd hoped Adderall would do for him, but he'd been plagued by the opposite effect.

Blake was lost in The World State when he heard Ms. DelGracio call his name again.

"Mr. Mitchell. I've received word that Mr. Greiner would like to speak with you in his office."

Perplexed as to why the principal would want to see him, Blake crinkled his nose and dog-eared his page in the book. "Should I bring my stuff, or will I be back in time to pick it up?"

"Bring your things," she answered, curtly.

As he exited the classroom, he could feel his peers' eyes on him. They were curious of what he had done, and Blake was wondering the same. Racking his brain while he walked to Mr. Greiner's office, Blake couldn't figure out what he could have done to warrant a meeting with the principal. He'd been on time for school and all his classes, he'd kept his head down and hadn't had any issues with his classmates, and he'd been respectful to his teachers. Everything was on the up and up.

"Take a seat, Blake," Mr. Greiner's administrative assistant directed as soon as Blake entered the office.

He did as he was told, his legs bouncing while he continued to theorize what he could have done. Peeking over his shoulder, he tried to get a view of what was going on in the principal's office through the small window beside his door. When he couldn't see anything but a pair of shiny black boots, he turned around and focused his attention on his fidgeting hands. Mr. Greiner wouldn't wear boots. Who was in there wearing boots? He glanced over his shoulder again, noticing that the black boots had a pair of perfectly hemmed navy-blue trousers resting on them. Fuck. It couldn't be, could it? Why the hell was he getting called to principal's office and why was the school resource officer seemingly awaiting his arrival? Regardless of what was going on, Blake wasn't feeling good about it.

"Blake," Mr. Greiner said from the doorway of his office. He waved Blake in, and dutifully Blake got up, ready to find out what the fuck was going on. "Take a seat," the principal ordered as Blake walked in.

Blake did as he was told, painfully aware of the fact that the SRO was standing in the corner of the room and that it wasn't a good sign of things to come.

"Do you recognize this bag?" Mr. Greiner asked, holding Blake's drawstring knapsack up as if it was on display.

Blake opened his mouth, not sure if he should admit that it was his bag or deny that he'd ever seen it.

"Before you say anything," Mr. Greiner interjected, "we know that this is your bag. Among other things," he grimaced, "we found your school issued iPad. It was returned to us and when the barcode was scanned it was yours."

Blake nodded, as he did mental gymnastics in an attempt to come up with a story that would explain what his iPad was doing among the illegal substances in the bag. He usually had the ability to think quickly on his feet, but the company was making him understandably flustered.

"So Blake, I'll ask you to confirm what we already know, and you'll get one chance before things get markedly worse for you," Mr. Greiner warned. "Is this your bag?"

"Yeah," Blake admitted, knowing the implications of the confession.

"And this is yours as well?" Mr. Greiner clarified, holding up a pipe and baggie of weed.

Peeking nervously at the SRO, Blake nodded. "Yeah."

While he was aware that the amount of weed wouldn't get him an intent charge, Blake could feel waves of anxious heat crashing over his body. A drug charge was the last thing he needed. Not only was his mother going to kill him, but he was an adult and could now be sentenced as one.

"Suffice to say you will be expelled from Woodland County High School. I'll receive confirmation from the board after their meeting on Thursday, and after that you'll no longer be permitted to attend this school," Mr. Greiner explained, "and aside from that, I'm unsure of your fate. That will be up to Officer Porter and the state of Kentucky."

Blake gnawed on the inside of his cheek so intensely that he could taste the metallic tinge of blood in his mouth. He was fucked. Super fucked. Epically fucked. He'd woken up that morning thinking that it would be a normal day, or what had become typical over the last few months, and the day had been anything but. His mother was going to kill him, and if she didn't kill him, she was going to disown him or do something similarly drastic. Not only would she be pissed about the weed after last March's car accident, but the expulsion would no doubt push her over the edge. She was tired, mentally and physically. It was obvious from her apparent exhaustion that raising Blake had been a doozy of a task. He wished he would've made it easier on her, shit like middle of the night drives into ditches and exposed stash spots hadn't happened, but that wasn't how things had shaken down. He tried to imagine what her face would look like when he told her that he'd been expelled. Even the thought of it was too much to deal with when the principal and SRO were in front of him, aggravated by his mere existence.

"Okay," Blake muttered, overwhelmed by the intensity of the whole scene.

"I assure you none of this is okay," Officer Porter chimed in, every ounce the intimidating douchebag. "There's a drug epidemic in Unionville and we've adopted a zero-tolerance policy."

Blake wanted to ask if such a low-population town had enough people to be considered an epidemic. He figured there was some sort of cut-off that Unionville wouldn't even approach. It also floored him that marijuana could be regarded as a problem at all. Who didn't smoke weed? It was natural, and awesome, and a lot less problematic than alcohol. Officer Porter probably toked over the weekend with the confiscated weed. He didn't put it past the squad to do shit like that, while threatening to mess with Blake's future.

"Would you like to say anything in your defense?" Mr. Greiner asked, pen in hand, ready to take notes.

"Am I under arrest?" Blake questioned, trying to control the fear in his tone.

"Not yet," Officer Porter answered, "but that doesn't mean you won't be."

"Something to look forward to then," Blake mumbled, shaking his head.

"I don't think there's much of that to be had for you," Mr. Greiner tsked, closing Blake's file. "You were doing so well, and now..."

"I'm still doing well," Blake interrupted. "Scholastically. Will my grades transfer?"

"First quarter grades have already been reported, so they will transfer to another high school if you do," Mr. Greiner answered. "I have to say, I'm surprised you're considering continuing. I didn't take you for the type."

"Well, you don't know me," Blake snarked, reaching for his bag. "Can I go now?"

Mr. Greiner peeked into the bag, as if to ensure there was no other illegal paraphernalia before handing it to Blake.

"I'll be in touch," Officer Porter commented, as Blake walked toward the door.

"I'd say I was looking forward to hearing from you, but I'm definitely not."

"I don't take that personally."

Blake nodded, thinking maybe he should.

16

In order to escape possession charges, and his mother's wrath, Blake found himself in an inpatient rehabilitation center in Lexington. It seemed that, like him, most patients at Brighter Horizons Substance Abuse Treatment Facilities didn't think they had a drug problem. Blake was convinced that they probably did, and he still didn't. Though it was illegal, weed was hardly a substance worthy of treatment. As he sat in meeting after meeting surrounded by grown-ass men and women who had ruined their relationships with spouses, children and family due to their addictions, Blake reaffirmed his commitment never to fuck with Adderall or the like again. He was sure he wasn't in need of rehab, but it was a good reminder of what could happen if he didn't watch himself in the future.

The length of the program was three weeks, but Blake completed it in two. He'd learned the acceptable answers and participated in every meeting and "good time" opportunity, building trust with the counselors and administration alike. All he wanted to do was go home, back to Unionville, back to his mom, to Greg, to sporadic moments of reconnecting with Claire. For years he'd dreamed of leaving his hometown, but now he yearned to return. Unfortunately, a homecoming wasn't in the cards.

Blake's psychologist was able to pull some strings and get him into a halfway house down the street from Brighter Horizons. Though he was eighteen and could make decisions for himself, Grace's insistence that he stay there rather than coming home had made the choice clear. While Blake didn't think his mother would throw him out on the street, he knew better than to test her after the shit he'd put her through over the last few years. The plan was that he'd stay in the halfway house and attend high school in Lexington until graduation, and then he was on his own.

The house was nice enough, aside from the fact that Blake had to share a room with a forty-year-old man who complained like he was ninety. Thanks to Ralph's presence, Blake tried to spend as much time as he could outside. Lucky for him, the weather was temperate for November, and the house had several bikes for the residents to ride as an initiative to promote physical activity and mental balance. Blake took advantage of the program, getting out on the bike as often as possible.

Sitting on a pedway, Blake watched as rush hour traffic crawled beneath him and considered how different his life would have been if Xander hadn't outed him sophomore year. There was no doubt he would still be on the wrestling team, but would everything else have truly been as disparate as he imagined? Chances are he would have continued to smoke weed, so he could have found himself in exactly the same situation he was now in, regardless of his extracurricular affiliation. Maybe there was a lesson to learn, one that he hadn't been able to identify yet. It was better to think that there was a reason for everything, than consider that there was no rhyme or reason behind his shitty luck.

Glancing at his phone screen to check the time, Blake was happy to see a text message from Greg.

Greg (6:15pm): How goes it playa?
Blake (6:18pm): Playa?
Greg (6:18pm): Playerrr?
Blake (6:19pm): No
Greg (6:19pm): Maybe?

Blake (6:19pm): No

Greg (6:20pm): How goes it Mitchell?

Blake (6:20pm): It goes. I'm watching traffic.

Greg (6:21pm): Badass. I'm watching paint dry. Tonight is lit.

Greg (6:22pm): When are you coming home?

Blake (6:23pm): May or June probably.

Greg (6:23pm): But you'll visit before then won't you?

Blake (6:24pm): Probably not.

Greg (6:24pm): Can I come up there or is it like prison?

Blake (6:25pm): It's not like prison. I can ask the house director and see what the rules are.

Greg (6:25pm): Cool. Let me know.

Blake (6:26pm): Will do.

Standing up and climbing onto the bike, Blake began to pedal in the general direction of the house, though he was becoming increasingly unfamiliar with his surroundings after taking what he thought was a correct turn.

"Shit," he grumbled as he continued further off-course. Racking his brain to remember the address, Blake tried typing a few options into his GPS, disappointed when none worked. He was about to plug in Brighter Horizons when his screen went black. Dead battery.

As he rode, getting more lost by the moment, the sky continued to grow darker. It was becoming evident that he wasn't going to make it home before curfew. During his orientation, the director, Mr. Trasker, had made it clear that there was no tolerance for breaking curfew, and that doing so would lead to removal from the program. The last thing Blake needed was to get kicked out of the halfway house. There would be no going home after that.

The sight of a police station in the distance had Blake riding faster, knowing that he would be able to ask for help. Jumping off his bike, he pounded on the door, hoping an officer could get him to the house in time.

"How can I help you?" a cop asked gruffly as he looked Blake up and down.

"Um, I'm lost. I'm staying at a halfway house on Lafayette and I can't seem to find my way back there," Blake explained, adjusting his glasses as he remained under the police officer's skeptical appraisal.

"How long have you lived there?"

"A couple weeks."

"A couple weeks," he repeated with a sniff. "You've been there a couple weeks and you're lost?"

"Yeah," Blake replied, knowing the cop was suspicious that there was more at play than he was admitting.

"And why are you in a halfway house, son? Were you incarcerated prior or were you in a treatment facility?"

"I was in a treatment facility," Blake confessed. "For drugs."

"Hmm, and are you under the influence right now?"

Blake shook his head vehemently. "Absolutely not."

"But you're lost, after being here a 'couple weeks...'" the police officer reminded him, as if he'd forgotten the pickle he'd gotten himself into.

"Correct," Blake answered. "Because I got turned around, not because I'm messed up."

"We'll see about that," the cop nodded, gesturing for Blake to follow him to a patrol vehicle in the parking lot. He helped Blake secure the bike to the rack on the rear of the car and told him, "Get in."

One look at the clock on the dash had Blake feeling sick. Seven-forty-five. By the time they got back it would be nearly eight, and he would be an hour past curfew. He hoped his sober state and the fact that he'd gone to the police for help would earn him some leniency or an exception.

The cop was quiet as he drove, which made Blake even more anxious. Though he'd gotten into a fair amount of trouble in the past, he'd never been in a police car. It was unnerving to think that instead of riding in the front, some of his actions could have landed him in the back.

The police station wasn't far from the house, which had Blake even more confused because he was positive he'd been further away.

"Thank you," he said, opening the car door before retrieving his bike. He was disappointed to see the officer getting out as well. He knew a police escort to the door would have his housemates and Mr. Trasker thinking the worst. He'd hoped that he could have simply informed the director about what had happened, but it seemed the cop had other ideas.

"I have a key," Blake said when the police officer stopped on the porch and knocked on the door.

"We'll do it the formal way."

Blake shoved his hands into his pockets and waited for inevitable.

A twitchy woman named Barbara answered the door, immediately screaming, "Trasker!" when she caught sight of Blake and his company.

A second later, the big man appeared, glaring at Blake while shaking hands with the cop. "Good to see you, Ted. What do you have here?"

"He says he's one of yours. The story is that he got lost and came to us to get him home."

"Lost?" Trasker asked, narrowing his eyes. "You've been here for two weeks, Blake."

"I know. I got confused. All the streets look the same."

"What were you doing out for so long to begin with?" Mr. Trasker questioned.

"Riding the bike, thinking. I don't know, regular stuff," Blake replied.

"Well, first thing's first," the director said, waving both men into the house. "We'll grab a urine sample to make sure you don't have any drugs in your system. You'll hang around for the results, Ted?"

"Absolutely," the officer nodded, taking a seat on the couch.

Blake sighed when Trasker disappeared into the powder room and came back with a drug test.

"Piss in the cup and leave it in there on the sink. I'll test it and we'll figure out if your confusion was chemically induced."

"It wasn't," Blake said firmly.

"No offense, but drug addicts aren't known to be pillars of truth," Mr. Trasker retorted.

Drug addict? Blake couldn't believe that anyone could so casually call him a *drug addict*. He went into the bathroom to take a leak, trying not to leak tears as he did. He felt exposed in a way he hadn't experienced before. Doing as he was told, he left the sample in the bathroom, washed his hands, and rejoined the police officer, Trasker, and a few onlookers in the living room.

It took a few minutes for Mr. Trasker to run the tests and report the findings Blake knew he would.

"He's clean," the director announced.

Evidently, that was the officer's cue to fuck off, which he did, leaving Blake to deal with Trasker and his broken curfew.

"We have a zero-excuse policy for tardiness," Mr. Trasker reminded, "which means tonight will be your last night as a resident of this house."

"Are you serious?" Blake cried, his heart pounding rapidly in his chest. "No excuses even when they're valid?"

"Zero-excuse policy," he reiterated, coolly.

"What am I supposed to do?" Blake asked, his voice wavering with emotion.

The older man shrugged. "That's your problem, not mine."

Blake inhaled deeply before letting out a sputtering exhale. He had enough problems. He didn't need this one.

17

Blake's first night in the homeless shelter was horrible. The place stunk like piss and dust, with a mustiness permeating every blanket and cot, making items that were bone dry feel damp. Before, Blake's mistakes had never been so tangible, but lying on the springy surface of the shelter cot, he couldn't avoid the discomfort of his new reality. It was cold, since the shoddy HVAC system was no match for the chill in the winter air. While theoretically Blake knew he was lucky to have a place to sleep that was indoors and relatively safe, it was hard to feel anything but defeated. How had everything gone so wrong?

Holding his belongings tight to his chest, Blake barely slept, protecting his things from sticky fingers that were ready to take them. Desperation was a powerful motivator and the shelter was rife with need. It would be tempting fate to let his guard down or allow his mind to rest.

It was strange to be in a position he never imagined himself in. Many times, Blake had daydreamed that he won the State championship for wrestling or became the valedictorian of his senior class. Sometimes he was in college, or a famous actor, but in all his wildest fantasies, he was never a homeless man. He'd never considered that one day he could be in a place like the one he was in, surrounded by people who had struggles he'd been blessed to never face. He wondered how many of them had a mother who cried herself to sleep every night worried about them, or a brother who was more than willing to give them guff, only because they cared. They probably didn't have a Greg, who rooted for them despite the mistakes they made, or a Claire, who they felt fulfilled by, even if they only had bobs and bits of a relationship.

If Blake would have found himself in the shelter after the car crash, he would have understood his lot, felt like he earned the punishment, but it was hard for him to rationalize why, after an innocent mistake, he was lying among the brutally mistaken, those who had sacrificed their lives for their vices. He didn't want to be like them, he hardly wanted to be like himself.

It was the morning after night two that Blake knew he had to do something to get out of the shithole. He thought about going back to Unionville and staying with Greg, but he knew it would be a hard sell to his friend's parents and that he couldn't attend WCHS again. He needed to find a place to stay that was in a different district. His top priority was to graduate, and he couldn't do that in a shelter or in his hometown. Knowing exactly who he needed to call, Blake made his way to the phone in the lobby, keeping his cell phone tucked safely in his pocket. He didn't want to draw attention to the fact that he had one.

It had been so long since he'd spoken to Ryan, and even longer since he'd spoken to Ryan's mother, Sandra. Blake missed them, and not only because it was looking like they were his last chance at a normal life. They lived in Jasmine County, a farming community thirty miles southwest of Lexington, a place where Blake knew he would have the ability to focus on finishing his senior year. Though his goals weren't far-fetched, they felt like they may be as he crossed the lobby floor. As sad as it was, nobody expected anything from the shelter's residents. He wondered how many of them knew differently about themselves like he did, how many saw beyond the societal views and reconsidered their own potential. Maybe it was true when people said that success took sacrifice. After all, Blake was sacrificing his pride to get in touch with a friend from fourth grade to ask him for a favor.

"Ryan?" Blake asked when a guy answered the landline with a standard hello.

"This is Ryan," he confirmed.

"Hey, it's Blake."

"Mitchell?"

"Do you know another Blake?" he laughed.

"I hardly know one," Ryan ribbed.

"That's fair," Blake sighed. "I should've been better at keeping in touch."

"It takes two," Ryan assured. "How have you been?"

"You know, okay," Blake lied, tapping his fingers on the desk as a man walked passed him, his clothing brushing against Blake's, too close, an invasion of space. "Is your mom around? I should probably talk to your mom?"

"Uh, yeah, hold on a minute," Ryan uttered.

Though Blake couldn't see his old friend's face, he could visualize it. There were years and miles between them, but Facebook had softened the impact of the distance.

"Sunshine?" Sandra exclaimed when she came to the phone. "Is that really you?"

"It's really me," Blake answered, smiling at the nickname. It had been so long since he'd heard it.

Although he didn't think of Sandra often, hearing her voice brought back warm memories of their time together. Blake had spent a significant amount of time at the Dempsey house growing up, and much of it was sitting at the kitchen table with Sandra, listening to her stories and telling her his. Though he was only nine, Sandra treated him like a young man, making Blake believe that his words and thoughts mattered. He hoped he did the same for her.

"It's been so long. How are you doing, Blake?"

"I've been better," he admitted, clearing his throat in an attempt to swallow the rising emotion.

"What's going on?" For every ounce of fear in his voice there were three more of worry in hers.

"So much," he sniffed, willing his eyes to hold in the tears that were threatening to spill from them. "I don't even know where to start."

"Start at the end and work your way to the beginning."

"I need a place to stay. I got in some trouble and I'm in a shelter right now."

"Oh honey," she sighed. "What kind of trouble?"

"Weed. I was expelled from school, went to rehab and then to a halfway house," Blake confessed, thinking the words sounded alien coming from his mouth. It was one thing to live the bizarre life he was living, but it was another to acknowledge that it was his.

"And why aren't you at the halfway house now?"

"I got kicked out. I was riding a bike, got lost, and missed curfew. That was it. One mistake and I was done."

"Were you out doing drugs?" Sandra asked.

"No, not at all. They gave me a drug test when I got back. I'll give you the director's name and he'll confirm I was clean. I missed curfew, that's it," Blake promised.

"You would have a curfew here, Sunshine, and I wouldn't take kindly to you missing it."

Blake had never been so relieved to receive a warning. "I swear I'd never miss it. All I want to do is go to school and graduate. That's it."

"That would be my expectation. You go to school, you stay out of trouble, and you keep the drugs out of my house. Ryan's doing well."

"I don't doubt it," Blake said. "You're a great mom."

"You don't have to butter me up, Sunshine. I'm already telling you that you have a place to stay."

"I said it because it's true," he replied, earnestly. "Thank you, Sandy."

"You won't thank me when you get your chore list," she joked, with her signature giggle.

"I still will," Blake laughed. "Believe me."

"Now, tell me where you are, and I'll come and get you after work."

"I'll probably try to go somewhere else today. How about you pick me up by Triangle Park? I'll stand at the corner of Main and Broadway."

"Sounds good," Sandra confirmed. "I'll be there around five-thirty, maybe a little later if traffic is bad."

"Take your time," Blake said, easily. "I'll be there."

"I'll see you later. We're having biscuits and gravy for dinner, so I hope you have an appetite."

Blake inhaled as the tears began to well again. He was hungry, but it was powerful how a show of kindness could be so fulfilling. "I have a big one."

"Then I'll make sure we have seconds."

She hung up, but Blake kept the phone pressed to his ear for a moment, relishing in the tenderness of the conversation for a bit longer.

"It's my turn," a man stated gruffly from behind Blake. "Get off."

"I'm off," Blake said, hanging up the receiver quickly. He couldn't wait to get out of there.

Power walking to the cafeteria, Blake found Pastor John handing out apples and government cheese.

"Pastor John, I wanted to thank you for all you've done. I found a place to stay."

"I'm happy to hear that, Blake," the white-haired clergyman smiled. "I hope you go with faith wherever you travel."

"Thanks," Blake replied, still impressed that the old man managed to remember everyone's names, even those who were new to the shelter.

"Apple?" the pastor offered, holding out the fruit.

Blake grinned and took it, grateful to have something to put in his stomach until he could fill it with Sandra's cooking later that night.

Exiting the shelter, Blake considered calling his mother and telling her what happened with the halfway house, but ultimately, he decided against it, knowing that her disappointment would be too much to bear. As he made his way toward State Street, he thought of calling his father, too. While he wasn't sure what his dad was doing or where he was, he knew for a fact he was busy. It had been so long since he'd spoken to him and it was an exhausting prospect to think of explaining all that had occurred. So, he decided not to. Instead he kept his head down and continued on his way, unsure of where he was going, but intent on never going back to where he'd been.

18

Settling into the Dempsey house was as easy as Blake had expected it to be. Ryan and Sandra radiated a positivity that Blake feared he'd forgotten how to muster. Regardless of how much he wanted to look past the things that had happened, Blake couldn't help but perseverate on his inability to stay out of trouble. He'd gotten lost in Lexington and promptly lost the opportunity he had to finish school in the city. It was a freak happening and it would be a permanent imprint on a pivotal page of his life. Maybe it was an analogy for some greater struggle, or perhaps he was an unlucky motherfucker. Either way, he still couldn't believe it had gone down the way it did. It didn't matter anyway; sleeping on the couch in Sandra's apartment was more comfortable than the halfway house, mostly because of the company. It was as if no time had passed between him and Ryan, and Blake was sure he'd feel forever bonded to Sandra, just because she was a salt of the Earth kind of person. Not only did he want to do well for himself, but he wanted to make Sandra proud, and his mother, though she wasn't aware of how far left shit had gone. He needed to focus on school and getting his diploma. Blake wasn't going to let circumstances and bad decisions stand in the way of his progress.

As expected, Ryan was a great influence. His old friend wasn't perfect, but he was pretty fucking close. He managed his school work, participated in track and field, and volunteered with elementary school kids on his afternoons off. Somehow, he managed to make time to let loose on the weekends and play a massive amount of video games, which made Blake happy as hell. While he wasn't interested in indulging too heavily in old habits, Blake wanted to blow off steam and he found that getting lost in a video game with his old friend was just what he needed. He couldn't deny that things with Nick had gotten out of control the year prior, but he was past the need to numb, and focused on lighthearted fun.

Blake found, however, that there was less opportunity to partake in the physical variety of the fun he was craving. There wasn't anybody at Jasmine County House School that interested him as much as Claire did, and there surely wasn't a gaggle of gay or bi guys openly looking to bang. Sexual frustration was at a peak, which was problematic given his very open sleeping arrangement. Blake never took more showers in his life. Something had to give and hopefully that something was a someone, ready to give him head.

"So, you like both guys and girls equally?" Ryan attempted to clarify as he and Blake sat in the park after school.

"Yes."

"I always thought if a guy fucked around with guys he was gay," Ryan admitted, "but I guess that's not the case."

Blake shook his head. It never ceased to surprise him how little people understood about bisexuality, but he could get why it was confusing for someone who grew up relatively sheltered by the conservative ideals of a red state like Ryan had. "I fuck around with girls, too. Would you consider me straight?"

"Not if you mess with dudes."

"Right, so I'm bi. Both," Blake reiterated, grinning at his friend. "It's nice to not have just one side, I guess."

Ryan nodded as if he was trying to process the information. "Sorry if I'm asking dumb questions, man, but I think I have another one."

"I don't care, Ry," Blake said nonchalantly. "What have you got?"

"You're only attracted to certain guys, right? Similar to how I'm only into certain girls?"

Blake flicked the paper or his cigarette, watching as the shimmering embers disintegrated before hitting the grass. "Exactly like that. I'm only into certain girls and guys. Being bi doesn't mean I want to fuck everyone. It's more that I want to fuck some people of both sexes."

"This is fascinating stuff," Ryan noted. "I thought long and hard about whether I've ever been into guys when you told me this bi stuff."

"Oh yeah?" Blake asked, raising his eyebrows in interest. "What did you come up with?"

"I'm straight," Ryan sighed. "I tried to imagine being with a guy and I couldn't get into the image."

"You know, I have to give it up to you for the effort. A lot of guys are too uptight to explore the option, even in their thoughts."

"I don't care what people say. There's something badass about getting a dick shoved up your ass."

"I don't really do that," Blake confessed. "I mostly top guys."

"Well, the guys you top are badasses then," Ryan laughed. "I'm not gonna give you the credit if it's not where it's due."

"Since when is sex a competition? They enjoy it just as much as I do. Believe me."

"You've always been cocky, Mitchell."

"Yeah well, my cockiness swelled with age," Blake joked, grinning when Ryan's hazel eyes went wide. "What? You opened it right up for that one."

"I did," Ryan laughed, reclining to his back.

Blake took the cue and laid next to him, staring up at the dense clouds creating a stratified grey sky. He wondered how long they had until they'd be walking home wet. Winter had been harsh in circumstance but not in weather, and Blake was still waiting for the snow that never came, only rain.

"Are you into me?" Ryan asked softly.

It was a fact of life that every time a straight male friend found out that Blake was bi they asked if he was interested in them. Eventually, it stopped being annoying and became expected.

"Nah."

"Why not?"

The tone of the question reflected more disappointment than Blake had expected to hear.

"Do you want me to be?" Blake asked, propping himself up on an elbow in order to get a view of Ryan's face.

"No. I'm curious," he answered, busying his hands by picking dead blades of grass.

"I don't know why I'm not. Maybe because you're Ryan."

"What's wrong with being Ryan?" he asked defensively.

"Nothing," Blake chuckled. "It's hard to see you in any way other than how I did when we were kids."

"I'm not asking you to," Ryan said quickly. "I don't know. It feels like there's something wrong with me?"

"Because of what I said?" Blake questioned, surprised that a handsome, amazing man like Ryan could be insecure.

"No," Ryan promised. "No, no, no, no. I just don't have much luck with girls. I mean, I'd like to be with one, but none of them seem interested."

"Why?" Blake wondered out loud. "You're a good-looking guy. You're smart. You're nice..."

"I think that's it. The nice thing. Girls don't seem to want a nice guy. Do guys?"

Blake shrugged. "I don't know. I'm not an expert."

"I think it's the glasses. People assume you're an expert on a lot of things," Ryan teased. "Professor Mitchell."

"I like it," Blake smirked. "It has a ring to it."

"I think so," Ryan agreed.

"Are you a virgin?"

"Don't ask me shit like that. It's embarrassing!"

"Who's around?" Blake asked, holding his arms up to display the empty park. "You can be real with me."

Sighing, Ryan bit his lip. "I'm sure you already have your answer now."

"Seems like it. A girl in my Spanish class asked about you the other day."

"Oh yeah? Who?"

"Her Spanish name is Marisol or something. I think her name is Maya?"

"Maya Schwartz?" Ryan asked hopefully.

"I don't know. She's petite, blonde."

"What did she ask?"

"How we knew each other," Blake replied.

"She was asking about you then?"

"About us," Blake corrected. "And how we know each other."

"Hmm," Ryan hummed, nodding his head. He sat up and held his thighs to his chest, resting his chin on his knee, just like he did when they were younger. "Have you had sex with both guys and girls?"

"Yeah."

"I can't even fuck one."

"Don't settle," Blake directed. "It'll happen when it happens."

"That's deep," Ryan grinned. "Do you like sleeping with one more than the other?"

"I promise I don't have a preference. People can't wrap their heads around it, but I don't."

"That's wild," Ryan uttered, regarding Blake as if he was a medical miracle. "Good for you, Blake. Honestly, good for you."

Blake laughed, running his fingers through his hair.

"I think about the universe sometimes..." Ryan began, lying down again.

"You're not even high," Blake joked. "What are you doing thinking about shit like that?"

"I know, but maybe people like you, people who are more inclusive in who they can love, are the future, and people like me who can only love one sex in a romantic way are antiquated and bringing humankind down."

"That's heavy."

"You have a strong back, don't you? You can hold that weight."

"I don't know anymore," Blake confessed. "Every part of me feels weaker than it did a few weeks ago."

"I think you just need more sleep. Is the couch uncomfortable?"

"No, it's perfect."

"That's a lie," Ryan laughed.

"It's better than where I've been, believe me. I have no complaints. I couldn't be more grateful to you guys for taking me in."

"Well, I'm happy to have you around and I know my mom is, too," Ryan smiled, standing up to brush the dirt off his jeans. "Let's get home before the storm."

Blake rose to his feet and walked with Ryan to the only place that felt like home in a while.

19

The best thing about Jasmine County High School, aside from Ryan, was the fact that seniors who were eighteen-years-old were allowed to sign themselves out. Because it was a farming community, many of Blake's classmates worked the land with their parents. The policy benefitted the farmers, who didn't have to waste time coming to school to excuse their kids when they needed help. Instead, they contacted their children and expected their arrival as soon as was feasible for the student.

Though Blake didn't cultivate crops, he did maintain an interest in gathering weed, which he worked on smoking whenever possible. When he told Greg about his newfound freedom, his buddy didn't take the bait.

Blake (11:32am): Want to hear the craziest shit?

Greg (11:33am): Always

Blake (11:33am): If you're 18 JCHS lets you sign yourself out. You can leave school if you need to. All you have to do is go to the office and write your name down.

Greg (11:34am): I'm assuming you have to have a reason.

Blake (11:35am): I do. I'm gonna hang out with my friend who misses me a lot.

Greg (11:35am): Who's that?

Blake (11:36am): Fuck you. Seriously. How about today? Cut school at noon, get here at 1, and we can spend the afternoon hotboxing your car.

Greg (11:37am): We can do that after school.

Blake (11:38am): Not really. School's over at 3:15. It'll take you an hour to get here, and I have to be back to Sandra's by 5:30pm for dinner. It doesn't give us any time. You gotta come earlier.

Greg (11:39am): This is why the weekends work better. It's March. I have two more months. I'm not getting in trouble for ditching.

Blake (11:41am): Uggghhh

Greg (11:41am): I miss you too.

Blake couldn't blame him, but that didn't mean he didn't wish Greg would come to Jasmine and chill. Knowing he needed to contact someone who was no longer in high school, Blake decided to give Bianca a try.

Blake (11:52am): Hey B. What's up?

Bianca (11:54am): Hey Little B. Not much.

Blake (11:55am): Little B? I'm bigger than you.

Bianca (11:55am): In height only, you skinny motherfucker. What do you want?

Blake (11:56am): Do you work today?

Bianca (11:56am): Nope.

Blake (11:57am): You should come to Jasmine.

Bianca (11:58am): What's in Jasmine?

Blake (11:58am): Me.

Bianca (11:59am): What else?

Blake (11:59am): Weed.

Bianca (12:00pm): What time?

Blake (12:00pm): Now

Bianca (12:01pm): Did you drop out of school or something?

Blake (12:01pm): No, I can sign myself out. I guess it's a thing here.

Bianca (12:02pm): Interesting. Where should I meet you?

Blake (12:02pm): Pick me up in front of the school. Text me when you're here.

Bianca (12:03pm): See you soon.

Blake hadn't been in touch with his old friend since the summer when Claire reunited them. He had a good time hanging out with her. It was similar to how things were with Ryan. Time passed but they could pick up where they left off. He shouldn't have expected any different. Bianca was cool as hell, with a tell-it-like-it-is attitude and a sarcastic mouth. She graduated from WCHS two years earlier, and mostly worked nights doing security at an office building in Unionville. With Bianca being free most days, and Blake's lawful liberation, he figured they'd be spending more time together. He was looking forward to it.

If Blake left school at one, he'd have a good amount of time to hang out before he had to make it home for dinner, and he would only miss two classes: Spanish and P.E. After taking French for four years, Blake wasn't thrilled that his only option for a foreign language at JCHS was to enroll in Spanish One, but he was pleasantly surprised by how easy it was, given his knowledge of French. He was confident that he could miss a few classes and still ace every test he was given. It hardly seemed necessary to go to Spanish and P.E. day after day, especially when he had the option not to.

When Blake received the text message from Bianca announcing her arrival, he walked to the office, wrote his name on the sign-out sheet, and fucked off. It was exhilarating to exit the building on his own accord. It had been so long since he'd had any sense of autonomy. He loved it.

"Long time, no see," Bianca greeted, smiling when Blake leaned over to give her a hug.

"Too long," Blake agreed, buckling his seatbelt, and sighing into the seat. "This is awesome."

"You missed me that much, huh?"

"For sure," he confirmed. "Pull out of the lot and make a right. We'll go to the park at the end of the block."

"Alright," she nodded, doing as she was told. "So how is it living in the boonies?"

Blake laughed. "Like Unionville isn't?"

"Not like this. The whole town smells like cow shit."

"I don't notice it anymore."

"That's because you're one of them," Bianca whispered, her dark eyes wild in reaction to a brewing theory. "They're like pod people. They took you over. Am I next?"

"Weirdo," Blake chuckled, shaking his head. "What's new with you?"

"Same shit, different day," she said.

"Are you still with your girlfriend? What was her name? The one at UK?"

"McKenna. Eh, not really. The distance is tough, man."

"You have a car and Lexington is an hour away," Blake stated. "How is that even distance?"

"She's needy as fuck," Bianca tsked. "We'll see what happens when I move to Lexington next month."

"You're moving?" Blake asked, surprised. "When did that happen?"

"Sometime in the seven months we didn't talk," she replied with a smirk. "You're shitty at keeping in touch."

"No doubt," Blake agreed. "You're not great either."

"Oh, I'm the worst," Bianca confirmed, "but I'm here now."

"I said I had weed."

"You don't think I have my own?" she questioned, pursing her lips. "C'mon now, Little B. I came out here to see you."

"I'm not into this Little B thing."

"Did I ask you?" she grinned, turning into the park. "You need someone to take you under their wing."

"I already have someone who's doing that," Blake said, "that's why I'm in Jasmine."

"You can never have too many people who give a shit about you though, right?"

"Probably not."

They got out of the car and Blake led Bianca to his spot beyond the dilapidated playground, under the shade of a cluster of Oak trees.

It was as private as a public place could be and secret enough to feel like his own.

"Your humble abode?" Bianca joked, lowering her rotund body to the ground.

"My home away from my home away from home," Blake clarified, settling in next to her.

"Say that three times fast."

"No thanks," he laughed, packing weed into the bowl.

As alone as he often felt, Blake couldn't deny that he had many people around him. People that would step up even after time apart. He made a mental note not to forget that at times when his perceived isolation became too much to cope with. His mistakes, while significant, were mistakes. He didn't want to spend his life seeking redemption and thinking that his shitty circumstances were a punishment steered by karma's control. There had to be people who did worse things than Blake did and evaded consequences. He wondered if their guilt eventually consumed them. He wondered if his would ever subside. It was hard to pinpoint exactly which actions contributed to the waves of darkness he sometimes experienced, but he did know he wanted them gone. He needed an accomplishment to wash away the failure. It would be better when he graduated.

"Do you have a lot on your mind?" Bianca asked, verbally shaking Blake from his preoccupation.

"Yeah," he confessed, lighting the pipe and handing it to his friend for the first hit.

"Are we going to talk about it?"

He shook his head. "I don't think so. It's nothing specific. My life isn't going the way I thought it would, I guess."

Bianca coughed out some smoke and cleared her throat. "Did you think you'd be boring? Standard?" she questioned. "The only people who can predict exactly how their life will go are boring people, who never shake shit up and live the status quo. Cogs in the machine of conformity."

"Hmm," Blake mused, licking his lips. "So, is your life going the way you thought it would?"

"Are you asking me if I'm a basic bitch who's done everything that was expected of me?" she laughed. "Are you really asking me that?"

"And you don't ever feel like a fuck-up?"

"Not at all. No chance. I go to work, I make money, I rent my place, I pay taxes, I have friends who like me enough, and girls who like me more. Does that mean my parents are proud of who I am and shit I do?"

Blake shrugged.

"They're not," Bianca said, "but that doesn't mean I'm not doing the right things. Doing what's right for me is the right thing. We have one life. Would you really want to live it for someone else?"

"Well, when you put it that way," Blake uttered, wide-eyed at Bianca's intensity. "No. I wouldn't want to live someone else's vision of my life."

"What's your vision then?"

"I don't know I've always had bad vision."

Bianca chuckled and nodded her head. "Fair. You have time to think about it. There isn't much to do out here than think."

"True," Blake agreed. "Have you talked to Claire lately? How's she doing?"

"You have her phone number, don't you?" Bianca challenged.

"Things are weird. It's hard for her and it's hard for me. She wants to be single and I don't know what I want. It's less complicated if we don't talk."

Bianca hummed and took another hit.

"What do you know that you're not telling me?" Blake asked, noticing the flash of guilt in Bianca's eyes.

"Nothing."

"She's not single anymore?"

"I didn't say that."

"You didn't have to," Blake mumbled.

"Don't throw me under the bus."

"We don't talk."

"So, keep it that way for a while," Bianca suggested.

"I plan to," Blake assured her. "I have enough to deal with."

"But look how good things are now. You're in Cowshittsville, cutting class legally, and smoking a bowl with me. What could be better?" she grinned.

Blake smiled, and leaned against the thick trunk of the tree. "Not much."

20

The saying "too good to be true" existed because often things were exactly that. Blake should have known that anything exceedingly positive in his life would have a loophole. He wasn't a negative guy, but he was aware of how quickly shit could hit the fan. Unfortunately, he'd grown used to it thanks to the choices he made and the onslaught of ramifications he dealt with.

Upon being called to the principal's office, Blake began having flashbacks of the happenings at WCHS. As he walked down the hallway toward his fate, he reminded himself not to cop to anything. There was no stashed weed, crappy behavior, or missed work. Blake could confidently say that he hadn't done anything wrong. He needed to remember that when he stepped into the line of fire. He doubted that he was being called to the office for any reason other than a negative one. In his wildest dreams, the administration was ready to compliment him on his hard work, but Blake knew that was one hell of a stretch. School types didn't take the time to say good things when they could berate him with bad. It was about power for them, feeling good about themselves while they made teenagers who were offbeat feel wrong. There was no pride in independence when falling in line was what was accepted.

By the time Blake arrived at the front office, he was prepared for the worst, in whichever form it was delivered. When he was younger, Blake was summoned to the principal for positive reasons such as perfect attendance and honor roll. He wondered if the practice of praise was antiquated considering the indefinitely negative slant a jaunt to the administration held. Bianca was right about a lot of things, namely how much those in charge hated anyone who didn't conform. He wanted a different type of life than the one they had, one that didn't place him in a box and keep him there, bored and normal. He wanted more than that, and maybe people who didn't fault him for it. Was it really that wrong to want to be free? Perhaps it was the curse of being a teenager that made him believe he could live outside the limits of what was acceptable. That made him think there was room for more in life than monotony.

Blake sat on the edge of his seat as Ms. Hanes paced the length of the small room. Her movement made him nervous and he wished she would sit down.

"Do you know why I called you here today, Blake?" she asked, continuing her trek to nowhere.

"I'd say for a formal welcome, but I've already been here for a few months."

She paused and rolled her lips under her teeth in a way that would have been funny if Blake wasn't fearing what was about to come out of her mouth. "We're expelling you from Jasmine County High School."

The statement was so outlandish that Blake asked the principal to repeat it. It didn't sound any less preposterous the second time.

"Why?" he breathed. Of all the things he'd imagined her saying, that wasn't on the list. "Expelled?"

"You've been signing yourself out," Ms. Hanes explained, opening a file on her desk. "Over the last month, you've signed yourself out seven times."

"I thought that was acceptable as long as the student was eighteen. I'm eighteen, I'm eighteen so I thought it was okay," he sputtered, as he became more lightheaded by the moment. He had to be caught in a nightmare. He'd wake up soon.

"With reason," she clarified. "Seniors who sign themselves out present the office with a note of reason the following day, typically signed by a parent, doctor, or employer, and even then, they are only allowed six independent leaves per semester."

"Are you serious?" he cried. "The office ladies watched me sign out all those times and never said a word. I had no idea."

"The registrar gave you a student handbook when you enrolled," Ms. Hanes reminded. "Part of being a responsible adult is doing your due diligence, Blake. You failed to do yours."

"I'll never do it again," Blake promised. "I'll have perfect attendance until graduation. I'll go to Saturday school to make up the missed hours." He was begging. He couldn't believe he was begging, but he was. He was begging, and from the stoic look on the principal's face, it wasn't working. "Please."

"Policy is policy," she said. "Good luck to you."

No mercy.

Leaving the school, it was difficult to rationalize that it would be his last time in Jasmine County High School or high school in general. There was no way another one would take him after being expelled from two. He lit a cigarette as he crossed the parking lot, feeling that if he were to peer over his shoulder he would see the school engulfed in flames. He'd burned everything down, every opportunity, every hope. A life on fire.

As he walked, Blake considered what he would tell Sandra, fearing how she would react. What if she kicked him out? She'd been clear in her terms. In order to live in the Dempsey house, Blake needed to be in school. He needed to be responsible. He needed to not fuck up the way he had. Afternoons with Bianca lost their luster, gleaming memories suddenly dulled by consequence. No joy, even that which was experienced in the past, shimmered in the shadow of failure.

"I really miffed it," Blake confessed as he sat at the kitchen table with Sandra and Ryan.

"Miffed what?" Ryan garbled, his mouth full of chicken.

Blake glanced at Sandra, who was regarding him suspiciously. Waiting. He cleared his throat, sniffed, and pushed his glasses up on the bridge of his nose, just about every one of his nervous ticks in a seemingly choreographed combination. "I got expelled."

"Come again?" Sandra said as Ryan dropped his fork to his plate with a clank.

"I got expelled. I heard that seniors could sign themselves out, so I did. One too many times I guess," Blake explained, his eyes fixed on Sandra's. "I asked for another chance, but she made up her mind."

"Well, this is a problem," Sandra sighed, removing the napkin from her lap and placing it on the table. She stood up and walked to the sink where she washed her hands, a tell of her mounting stress. "Hmm."

"Really?" Ryan whispered.

Blake nodded, placing the heel of his hand on his chin as his fingers tapped his nose.

"Fuck."

"Yeah, I'm not happy about it," Blake promised with a sardonic laugh. "At all."

"So, what are we going to do about this?" Sandra asked, drying her hands with a dish towel before returning to the table. "Part of the deal was that you'd be in school."

"I know," Blake replied, his stomach dropping to his ass.

Sandra was going to kick him out. After finally settling in some-where that made him happy, he would be back on the street. The thought alone was enough to have his stomach gurgling and bile rising in his throat. He didn't want to go to the shelter, and there was no way he could show his face in Unionville. Blake had told his mother he was doing well, that he was on track to graduate. She sounded proud. He didn't want to take that away from her, from himself.

"You'll have to get a job," Sandra decided.

Both Blake and Ryan exhaled their relief. It hadn't been what Blake was expecting, and evidently it was a surprise to Ryan, too.

"Thank you," Blake said, jumping up from his chair to give Sandra a hug. "I'll find something right away. I'll contribute to the house, food, everything."

"I know you will, Sunshine," Sandra soothed, rubbing his back as she hugged him back. "You get yourself into some muck, don't you?"

"I do," Blake confirmed. "I have to break the cycle somehow."

"The best way to do that is to learn the rules and follow them."

"No matter how much they suck," Ryan added, beginning to eat his meal again. "You should've told me you were signing yourself out. I would've told you not to."

"I didn't think anything of it other than how awesome it was," Blake shrugged, as he sat down. "You always have practice or something else going on, so I figured you never took advantage of the opportunity."

"You're right about that, but I do know how it works. Maybe somewhere deep down you knew it was shady business," Ryan offered.

"You make it sound so intense. It wasn't like that, but damn was I excited about it."

"What did you do it anyway? When you left school? What did you do with your time?" Sandra asked, grimacing as if she didn't want to know the answer.

"I thought a lot about things," Blake replied. It wasn't a lie.

"Like how you should have been in class?" Ryan joked, earning him an unimpressed scowl from Blake. "Too soon?"

"Probably," Blake nodded, peaking at Sandra, who was still regarding him with narrowed eyes.

"I'm amending a portion of our agreement, but that certainly doesn't mean I'm willing to be lenient on any of the other terms," she stated. "Understood?"

"Understood."

"You can the bend rules, Sunshine, but there's rarely enough to prevent people from breaking if you push them too far. Don't push me too far. I'm not flexible."

Blake nodded. "Yes, ma'am."

She shuddered at the formality. "And don't 'ma'am' me."

"I won't 'ma'am' you," he laughed, taking a bite of his now cold dinner.

"You can 'sir' me," Ryan smirked. "I feel like I deserve that level of respect. I don't think enough people call me sir."

"I don't think anybody calls you sir and the trend isn't going to start with me," Blake assured his friend with a grin. "I'm beginning to think I have a problem with authority." He turned quickly to Sandra. "Not you, of course. You're a queen, Sandy."

"Now, queen," she paused, a large smile spreading across her lips, "queen I can work with. I like that."

"I like you," Blake said simply, exceedingly grateful that the Dempsey's were in his life.

"I like you, too, even though you're one heck of a handful."

"I've been called worse, but never by a better person," he replied, garnering a click of the tongue from Sandra.

"You're a charming one, Blake Mitchell."

"Too charming," Ryan opined, as he chewed on a hunk of bread. "It's the dimples."

"You know, I've been told that before," Blake mused, recalling how Greg used to poke his finger into the indentations in his cheeks. "Maybe it's a thing."

"Thanks for the dimples, Mom," Ryan said to Sandra, sarcastically.

"I could give you some," Sandra teased, holding her fork up. "Ready?"

"I'm good," Ryan chuckled. "Now that I think about it, I was made perfectly."

Blake agreed, knowing he had some work to do.

PART III

ADULTHOOD

21

In theory, Sandra's insistence that Blake get a job and contribute to the household made a lot of sense, but it practice, it wasn't so easy. Aside from farms, there was little to no commerce in Jasmine County, and without a car, Blake couldn't look for work too far from the Dempseys' place. It would have been great if there was a job he could do from home, but without a computer or a high school diploma that setup was unlikely. Instead of wasting Sandra's time— and his own—he worked out a plan to move in with Bianca in her new apartment in Lexington. He'd get a job in the city, where there were more opportunities, and start his life as an employed adult.

"I hate that you have to go," Sandra sighed as she parked in the lot outside of Bianca's building.

"He could stay," Ryan reminded his mother, garnering a click of the tongue and an unimpressed shake of the head from Sandra.

"You know I can't," Blake said, leaning forward from the backseat to pat his friend's shoulder. "It doesn't make any sense to stay. There's nothing for me in Jasmine."

"You sound like a drifter," Ryan laughed. "Am I never going to see you again? Is this it for us, are we sporadic for the next nine years like before?"

"No way. I'll be better about keeping in touch," Blake promised, hoping that he actually had the capacity to do so. He didn't forget about people when he fell off, but with his history of movement it was hard to stand still for long enough to nurture relationships.

"With both of us," Sandra added. "I want to hear wonderful updates from you. That you got your GED, a job, most importantly that you're happy, healthy..."

"I hope I have good things to share."

"You make things good. That's the only way to have good things. You make them good. You can't wait for it all to be figured out for you," Sandra told him passionately. "I want you to really hear what I'm telling you, Blake. I want it to go in."

"I hear you," Blake promised.

"And it's going in?"

Blake tapped the side of his head. "It's right here."

"Well, let's get out and do some hugging before you leave us," Sandra said, unlocking the car doors and climbing out.

Wrapping his arms around Ryan's shoulders, Blake held him close, a sadness he wished he could ignore pressing on his chest. He'd said goodbye to too many people over the last several months. He didn't want his life to be turbulent or variable anymore. He wanted something solid and consistent, to know that everything wasn't going to be ripped away from him because of a broken rule.

"It's been real," Blake grinned, tussling his friend's sandy blond hair. "Take care of yourself, or better yet, let your mom take care of you, she's good at that shit."

"She is, isn't she?" Ryan nodded, smiling at his mom. "Keep in touch, Blake. I'm not messing around."

"I will. I swear," Blake assured.

As he walked to Sandra, he dreaded the send-off. She squeezed him tight in a way that promised support and care. He wanted to be worthy of the affection. Maybe one day he would be. While Jasmine and Sandra didn't turn out to be the sturdy surrounding he craved, it was a good baseline for what he would strive toward in the future.

"It's been a pleasure. Don't be a stranger, alright?"

"I won't be. Thank you for everything, Sandy. You didn't have to take me in and you did. It means a lot."

"Oh hush," she huffed, pressing her knuckle against her now teary eyes. "I'm not made for this type of stuff. I'm too soft. You have to go before I flood the place and you'll need to travel by boat."

Blake nodded, grabbing his bag out of the trunk. He gave them one last wave and then headed into Bianca's building. Climbing the stairs to the third floor, he knocked on the door of apartment 342 and chuckled when his friend yelled, "It's your place, too, Little B. I'm on the couch. Let yourself in."

Doing as he was told, Blake was pleased to see Bianca lounging on the sofa with two joints and a pizza on the coffee table. "This housewarming party is lit," he grinned, dropping his bag on the worn carpet and sitting down next to Bianca.

"Don't get used to it. Your ass is buying next time," she stated. "I told you. No freeloading."

"No freeloading," Blake confirmed. "I'll start looking for a job tomorrow."

"I think I found something for you."

"Oh yeah?"

"Pizza?" she offered, opening the box to present the pepperoni pie to him.

Taking a slice, Blake muttered his "thanks" as the bubbling, hot cheese burned the roof of his mouth.

"Like it?"

He shrugged. "It's pizza and it's free. I have no complaints."

"It's from White Knight Pizza on Richmond. They're hiring. I told them you'd be in tomorrow afternoon to fill out an application."

"You work fast, Garza," Blake remarked with an impressed nod. "Is it a nice place.

"Hell no. It's a shithole. I actually think it may be a mob front, but whatever, you know, it's money. Rumor on the street is they pay under the table and don't give a damn what their employees do as long as they don't touch the till."

"I wouldn't touch the till," he said, reaching for another slice.

"Thanks for letting me know. Do you think I'll get a pizza discount?"

"I think we'll get really sick of pizza."

"Can that happen? Can people get sick of pizza?"

"I bet they can get sick of bad pizza. This is pretty bad," Bianca laughed. "I usually eat it when I'm already high. It's way worse when I don't have the munchies."

He raised his eyebrows and held up the joints. "A welcome gift?"

Bianca smirked. "You know me. The hostess with the mostest."

"Let's make the pizza taste better then," Blake grinned, placing a joint between his roommate's lips before lighting up his own. "Fuck," he sighed, tilting his head back as he coughed on the smoke. "This is pretty cool, right? You and me. Living in the city. Nobody to answer to, actual freedom."

"We're not free," she corrected. "Not even close."

"It feels like freedom to me."

"Freedom is not worrying about the utility bill or if you can go for a case of Bud instead of Natty. We're too poor to be free."

"We're not poor," Blake disagreed. "I've been around poor and it's not us."

Bianca chuckled. "That's your problem, Mitchell. You need to think of yourself as desperate. It's the only way you'll ever be hungry enough to tear people's throats out if they get in the way of your rise."

"You're intense as hell," Blake laughed, his eyes wide. "I'm applying for a job at a fucking pizza shop. Whose neck do I need to break to be a goddam pizza boy?"

"It's not pizza, B. It's survival. You'll see. You owe me half the rent next month. Handing over that money...you'll get it then."

"I'll have it," he affirmed, taking another hit. "You should give me the tour."

"There isn't much to show. This is the living room. That's the kitchen." She pointed to the galley kitchen in the back corner of the room. "My bedroom is on that side, and yours is there. The shitter is next to mine, but not attached because places like that are two-hundred dollars more a month. I got the second bedroom instead because I knew I'd find someone to live with."

"It's amazing. I haven't had any privacy in months. The fact that my room has a door," he sighed, "this is heaven to me." He looked longingly toward *his* room.

"You'll have to buy a bed if you want one, but I put an air mattress in there for now. How about you go check it out?" Bianca smirked, nudging Blake's knee with hers. "I won't be insulted. Do you, man. Relish it."

Blake didn't have to be told twice. Within seconds, he was in the small bedroom, door closed, lying on the bare AeroBed, smoking, emancipated. He needed to get sheets, but a comforter could wait. Summer was coming. He felt his lips turn up. He was going to be in the city for summer, meeting new people, living a different life than the one he lived before. Not only towns but worlds away from Unionville. Every mile was a margin, creating space.

Blake basked in the solitude. He'd miss Sandra and Ryan, but the promise Lexington held was intoxicating. An uncharacteristic giddiness began to flutter through his body. Maybe this was where he was supposed to end up after all the bullshit. Maybe his future was already written, and he wasn't privy to the script. He needed to embrace the change, hold onto moments of magic like the one he was existing in, alone in his first bedroom as an adult. He'd felt tethered by his mistakes, but he was ready to cut the cords of compunction and make something amazing of his life. It wasn't enough to *be* anymore, he wanted to be something more, someone more than the person he'd been. And now he had the chance. He wasn't going to fuck it up. He'd done enough of that. There was more to life than his reckless past. Perhaps a future full of fortitude he hadn't been able to gather.

Somehow the air in his new apartment felt different than the stale spaces he'd been breathing in for years prior. He wouldn't be defined by a small town or faults. He could be somebody else, or himself, but better, understood. It was only when everything was torn from you that you could look forward to grasping the things that mattered. He would stretch for something more. He had to.

22

W hite Knight Pizza was much more of a dumpster fire than Bianca had described. Upon entry, Blake regretted ever eating anything that had been produced in their kitchen. That didn't mean he didn't take the job when it was offered to him. He showed up dutifully day after day, and didn't ask questions, which was evidently the mark of a good employee to Tony and crew. Blake put pizza in boxes, took orders and ignored all other goings-on in the shop. While he wasn't sure—and couldn't deny—there was some criminal activity happening, Blake was getting paid under the table, which was shady in its own right. Still, he had no complaints. He was off the grid, a presumed high school student not earning an income and avoiding the responsibility of taxes. Someday soon he'd pay the government their due, but first he was concerned with getting his own, and giving it to Bianca for the apartment. His roommate had laid down the law and he wasn't about to fuck things up. The apartment was small and in moderate disrepair, but it had become his safe haven. He'd never loved anything unremarkable so intensely. It wasn't the bones of the apartment that attracted him, but the guts, what the place represented.

Like she did at her security job in Unionville, Bianca worked third shift at her new post in Lexington. Though Blake often worked nights as well, he loved the rare evening when he was off and had the apartment to himself. He walked around naked, blasted music, and relished in the privacy. There was no one to answer to, nobody judging his decisions, no sneaking in or out. He was where he was supposed to be. Finally, he believed that the erratic nonsense that plagued him was settling down, that there was a chance the shards of everything he'd broken could be pieced back together. A different picture with the same premise.

The first time Blake brought a guy back to *his* place was electric. He didn't have to worry about his mother getting home early from work or his brother's big mouth. He could focus on the hard body beneath him, the hands rubbing his back, the feet hooking his shins as he sunk deeper inside him. Thanks to the Rise and Grind, he was fulfilled physically, but the assembly line of men weren't fortifying him emotionally. The more sex he had, the more he wished he was having it with someone who stuck around in the morning, who wanted to talk about life and the future, who wanted someone to rely on, to be that person for someone else.

"Good morning, Princess," a man's voice whispered, waking Blake from a death-like slumber. He half expected to turn over and see a random guy on the air mattress next to him. Rolling to his side, Blake grinned when he realized the bedmate was anything but random.

"I thought you weren't coming till noon."

"I couldn't hold out," Greg replied, pinching Blake's cheek. "Do you think I'm gonna pop this float you're sleeping on?"

"It's not a float," Blake chuckled. "It's an AeroBed and it's survived the poundings I've put it through, so I think you're fine."

"You bring people back to your air mattress?" Greg teased.

"It's better than the couch I was sleeping on before," he said, leaning over to pick his glasses up off the nightstand.

"How do I look?"

"Better before."

"Asshole," Greg laughed, shaking his head.

"You animals should lock your door. Anybody can walk right in."

"I see that now."

"Do you know any good places for breakfast?"

"That depends on if you're buying or not," Blake replied.

"So, I drive an hour to see you and then get the honor of paying for your meal?"

"Honor of my company," Blake corrected, sitting up and stretching his arms over his head with an exaggerated groan. "Shit. What time is it anyway?" He glanced at his phone screen. "It's seventy-thirty, you prick! Who wakes up at seven-thirty on Saturday morning?"

"I was up at six to get ready and get here by seven-thirty. I'm productive as fuck. You gotta get like me, B."

"If getting like you means I have to get up at the ass-crack of dawn, I'll hold off on that," Blake decided. "I'll jump in the shower and then we can go."

"I want biscuits."

"You just looked at my butt and said that," Blake pointed out with a smirk.

"You're a monster," Greg stated, placing his hands behind his head. "Hurry up. I'm hungry."

Making his way to the bathroom, Blake expedited his morning routine as his stomach rumbled at the thought of a hearty breakfast sponsored by his best friend. By the time he was done, Greg had migrated from his bed to the living room couch.

"That shit's uncomfortable, man," he tsked as Blake put on his University of Kentucky hoodie. "Your back will be wrecked if you keep sleeping on it."

"You're really worried about this bed shit," Blake laughed. "I'm fine. My back's fine. The only thing that's not fine is my stomach since you mentioned biscuits."

"I Yelped a few restaurants around here, and a place called 'Josie's' looks promising."

"What're you a fifty-year-old woman? Who Yelps shit?"

"People who like good meals and dislike food poisoning. I go to the one-star ratings and word search 'poisoning' before I eat anywhere," Greg explained.

Blake froze in place to stare at his friend, searching for words that would properly express how fucking crazy he thought the statement was. When he couldn't come up with any, he shook his head slowly and uttered. "Come on."

"I like your sweatshirt," Greg noted as he and Blake ambled down Richmond toward Josie's.

"I've been wearing this one for years," Blake reminded him.

"I like it better now than I did before."

"Hmm," Blake hummed, lighting a cigarette and offering one to Greg, who took it and asked, "Do you want to know why?"

"I thought it was just because you were weird," Blake reasoned, grinning at Greg.

"I got in."

"To UK?" Blake questioned, stopping dead in his tracks to process the news. "You're going to UK?"

A wide smile brightened Greg's full face. "Yup. I was on the waiting list and I found out yesterday that it's a full acceptance."

"Wow," Blake breathed, closing his eyes for a moment as the early morning spring breeze fanned through his hair. Pulling up his hoodie, he reached out to shake his friend's hand. "Congratulations, Greg. That's incredible."

"My student loans are going to be bananas, but I'm looking forward to it. I'm proud of myself, you know?"

Blake nodded. He didn't, but he wanted to. While he was glad to have a job, he was hardly proud of his position at the shady shit shack where he worked. Greg was going to college, better yet, to UK, exactly where Blake had imagined himself attending. When wrestling was going well, Blake thought that he might have the chance at a scholarship, but those hopes were dashed long before his college dreams were. Though he tried, it was difficult for Blake to ignore the pangs of jealousy that poked his heart and made him feel like an asshole. "You should be."

"After you get your GED this summer you can apply for second semester," Greg suggested, as they began to stroll again.

Blake punched out a wry laugh. "Oh yeah! There's no doubt they would accept a guy with a GED and two high school expulsions under his belt. That ship has sailed, hit a reef, capsized and caught on fire."

"You really went hard on that analogy," Greg praised.

"Idiom," Blake informed him. "It's an idiom, not an analogy."

"This is why they'll take you, because you're smart."

Blake shrugged and focused on the nicotine he was pulling into his lungs.

They walked quietly for a few moments, until Greg remarked. "You're doing much better than your buddy Nick."

"What's going on with Nick?"

It had been so long since they'd spoken. While he liked Nick, it had been obvious to Blake after the car wreck that if he was going to turn things around, he needed to cut ties with him.

"He's in prison."

"No shit," Blake gasped. Though he wasn't entirely surprised by the news, considering he always figured Nick would wind up incarcerated, it was crazy to think he was actually in prison, doing time. "What did he do?"

"I think it was initially going to be solely a drug charge, but then the idiot supposedly resisted arrest and swung at an officer."

"Fuck, that's dumb, even for Nick."

"Your boy," Greg ribbed, earning a middle finger salute from Blake.

"You're my boy," he stated as they entered Josie's. The smell of bacon and syrup instantly had Blake's mouth watering.

"I'm more like your bitch. You order me around and I drove sixty miles to take you to breakfast."

"You said it, not me," Blake laughed, slapping his friend on the back.

"I've come to terms with what I am," Greg relented. "I own it like you own me."

"The drama...fuck," Blake chuckled, dodging the ear flick Greg tried to deliver. "Quit it."

"Table for two?" the hostess asked, her expression indicating she was unimpressed by their horseplay.

They nodded and followed her to a booth where she tossed the menus down and walked away.

"I think I'm that cranky at White Knight Pizza," Blake noted, sliding into the seat.

"I have no doubts," Greg said, taking his phone out of his pocket and typing feverishly.

"Are you fighting with somebody?" Blake asked, taken aback by his intensity.

"No. I'm making a list for my review."

"You write reviews, too?" Blake questioned, eyes wide.

"Of course I do," Greg replied easily.

Blake shook his head with amusement. Of course he did.

23

Blake had to wait until mid-June to take his GED, but he'd committed himself to taking a few classes at the library in preparation. After completing the test, Blake realized how unnecessary the brief preparation course had been. Not only had he done well, he'd completely annihilated it, which only made him wonder how he would have done on the SATs. He wanted his constant comparison of where he was and where he should have been to dissipate, but the thoughts never waned. Instead, his perseverance became more overpowering with every benchmark he reached. It was as if none of his achievements would ever be enough because of how far off-track he'd drifted. He knew he needed to come to terms with the change in path but working a low-paying job with not much to look forward to in terms of advancement made a positive spin impossible. While Bianca, Greg, and even his mom were praising his accomplishments, Blake couldn't see beyond his deficits. He needed to shift his perspective and go easier on himself, but he feared that in doing so he would revert back to old patterns. Maybe if he remained harsh on himself, he would continue to rise above the pervading feeling that nothing mattered now that he'd pissed away his chance at a high school diploma.

Greg continued to tell Blake that a GED didn't limit him from going to college in the future, but it was difficult for Blake to consider the cost of community college tuition with the amount of money he pulled in at White Knight Pizza. He needed to be on the other side of Tony's business model, the non-pizza portion where some big deals were going down. While the thought of easy money was appealing, Blake didn't want to do anything illegal. He was over getting into any type of trouble. He needed to stay legit, not only for his future, but for his present. He couldn't look in the mirror and continue to see how his disappointing decisions clouded his face. He wanted to see himself for who he knew he could be, not who he had been.

Nobody had given Blake a second-chance. In all of the situations when the book was thrown at him, there had been no benefit of a doubt or a warning. He'd always gotten the full extent of the punishment. He was the only person who would ever allow himself a second-chance, and still he obstructed his own path. Perhaps it had all happened how it did to test him. The universe's way to strengthen his resolve, to fill his spinal column with steel. He needed to be fiercer than his fear of constant failure. Knowing that was the majority of the battle. He didn't want to stop fighting for his future, to stop believing that he had the chance to have one that could be full of success.

"You've come so far," Grace told him after he called to tell her how his test had gone.

"You thought I'd be further by now. That I'd be headed to college, wrestling, doing a lot more than I'm doing now," Blake contested, rubbing his knuckle against his nostril as he sniffed away from the phone.

"Blake," she chided. "You're doing what you can with what you have. You're ambitious and driven. You'll get past all of this and make something of yourself. I know you will. I never doubted you once."

He laughed wetly at the assertion. "That's bullshit and you know it. You doubted me plenty junior year."

"I doubted who you'd become, but never who I knew you were."

The statement had Blake wondering if his mom was smoking

weed, but her aversion to all things fun assured him that wasn't the case. "That's deep, Mom."

"I have my moments."

"Don't we all," Blake muttered, letting his eyes climb the skyscraper in his vision line. The spire cut the blue sky, but the clouds remained whole, forming around the intrusion rather than fleeing.

"When are you going to come for a visit? I miss you. You're only an hour away but it feels like worlds."

"Soon," Blake promised, sure that he wouldn't follow through. Going back to Unionville was returning to a past he didn't want to claim, at least not yet. "You can come up here, too. I'll take you to dinner."

"You will?" Grace asked. He could tell she was smiling.

"I will. I make a few bucks. Literally, like, a few. I'll spend them on you."

"I'm honored, but I wouldn't let you."

"I mean, I'm not going to beg," Blake chuckled.

"I didn't imagine you would, my stubborn boy."

"How's your other boy?"

"Logan's good," Grace answered. "He's still working at the garage and he's close to becoming a full-fledged mechanic."

"That's great," Blake remarked. "Is he still with the girl with the kid?"

"He is. Brianna," she confirmed. "And his name is Owen and he's such a sweet kid. You'd really like him. You've always been so great with kids."

Unsure of what to say, Blake remained silent. Life was flying by him. Streaks of neon light stretching down endless corridors while he stood in the center of an empty hallway, motionless.

"It's crazy. If they get married, I'll be a step-Grandma. Can you imagine? A step-Grandma at my age?"

"How old are you again?" Blake teased.

"You're supposed to say based on looks alone you couldn't fathom it," Grace chided playfully.

"I didn't get the memo, and I haven't seen you in a while. I'm guessing I gave you some grey hairs over the past year."

"Oh plenty. I also have four new wrinkles with your name on them," she informed. "So maybe step-Grandma status isn't such a stretch."

"I'm sure you look great."

"If you come for a visit you can see how wrong you are."

"I love seeing how wrong I am," Blake joked. "I do it often."

"You know what I mean," Grace said with a click of her tongue. "Really. I'd love for you to come for dinner on one of your nights off."

His mother was persistent. Every time they spoke on the phone they had the same discussion, multiple times, in one conversation. It had come to the point where her pleas went in one ear and out the other. He could only take so much, especially about a topic that made him so uncomfortable.

"It's easier for you to come to Lexington like you did before. You have a car," he reminded.

"I'll absolutely come to the city, but you should consider coming to Unionville. You can't stay away forever."

"Who said anything about forever?" Blake sighed, aggravated with himself that he felt compelled to avoid his hometown.

"All I'm saying is that it's been a while, Blake."

"I get it. Like I said, I'll come home soon, for Thanksgiving or something."

"Thanksgiving is in..." Grace paused to count, "five months. How about we aim for before then?"

"Alright," Blake sighed. "Listen, I'm about to walk into work. I'll talk to you later."

"Okay, honey. Have a good night and be safe."

"Slinging pizzas?"

"Doing whatever you do," Grace asserted. "Slinging pizzas, walking home at night, hanging around with people...just be safe."

Blake uttered "goodbye," shoved his phone into his pocket, and pulled open the door to White Knight Pizza.

"You're late," Tony grunted as Blake hung his backpack on a hook in the kitchen and put his apron on.

"No, I'm not," Blake contested, pointing to the clock on the wall. "It's four-forty-five and I'm scheduled for five o' clock."

"Oh, well, good on you for being on time."

With that, he disappeared into his office, where he'd no doubt spend the rest of the evening receiving a smattering of suspicious visitors who barely looked Blake in the eye when they entered the shop.

"You're on phones and register tonight," Alfonzo stated.

Blake nodded, hung the apron back on its hook and walked to the front counter where he planted his ass on the stool and waited for the hours to drag by.

Sometime after ten, he answered the phone and heard a familiar voice attempting to disguise itself with an awful Australian accent.

"'ello, mate! How are you doin' on this fine evenin'?"

"You're already wasted, and I'm jealous," Blake told Bianca, who huffed in response.

"How did you know it was me?"

"That accent was horrible," he laughed. "I thought you were working tonight, too?"

"Nope. I'm off, and McKenna is over."

"Nice."

"We're hungry. What time are you done?"

"Eleven."

"Awesome. Bring home a pizza please."

"Is this an official order or a roommate request?"

"I don't want to pay for the thing," Bianca clarified. "If I wanted to pay, I'd call Pies and Pints and get something good."

"What's in it for me?" Blake asked, knowing full well he was going to bring his friend the pizza.

"Two cans of Bud and a big fat blunt, which exceeds the value of your pizza exponentially," she replied, reverting to her accent again.

Blake heard McKenna tell her girlfriend, "You don't even sound Australian. You sound like a Southerner attempting to do a shitty British accent."

"It doesn't turn you on?" Bianca asked. The question was followed by giggling and the sound of the phone sliding against skin.

"I'll bring it home," Blake said, though he suspected they'd already forgotten about the call.

"That sounded like a personal call," Alfonzo called from the kitchen. "You know what they say about personal calls, right? Have them on your own time."

Blake nodded, biting his tongue to keep the words, "you know what *they* say about money laundering," contained. White Knight Pizza sucked, but it was a steady trickle of money and he needed the job. He kept his head down, his mouth shut, and his stomach full of shitty pizza, and for the time being, it was enough.

24

Blake didn't think his job at White Knight Pizza could get any worse, and then came autumn. As co-eds descended on Lexington for the new school year, Blake's hours and the demands of the job increased. The counter was constantly crowded with drunk teenagers attempting to pay for their pizza with crumpled bills and gum, and he was over it. It wasn't that Blake couldn't handle their antics, that part was fine. There was something about University of Kentucky students scraping their last dollars together to buy crappy pizza from a possible mob cover that rubbed him the wrong way. Everything Tony and Alfonso did pissed him off. They were growing more acerbic by the day and Blake was having a hard time remaining pleasant toward them. Most of the time, he kept his mouth shut, but there were moments when it was painful not to snap back at them.

The idea of searching for a new job seemed overwhelming considering his lack of desire to commit to another low-income, dead-end position. Chances were, he'd grow to despise another place as much as he did White Knight Pizza. Still, it was difficult to take pride in a company that didn't take any pride in themselves. Prior to the pizza shop, Blake hadn't had much work experience, so he'd never known how important it was to feel like there was some purpose behind what he was doing, that he was learning useful skills or somehow bettering himself. The only thing he was doing was rotting.

"I'm off," he told Alfonso as soon as the clock struck nine.

"What time are you scheduled to work until?"

"Nine. That's why I'm leaving," Blake said slowly, "because that's what time I'm scheduled until, and it's nine."

"You should've been scheduled until eleven. It's Friday and we're busy," Alfonso said, pushing a pie into the oven. "You're going to have to stay until at least eleven."

"If I should've been scheduled until eleven, then you should've had me scheduled until eleven.

"Well, I'm scheduling you now until eleven. Would you like me to get Tony to sign off on the change, or do you feel confident in my directive?" Alfonso threatened, narrowing eyes at Blake.

Rage ignited in his body, building in his chest and splaying to his limbs, urging him to throw a punch or leave the restaurant, but he did neither. Instead, he walked back to the counter and took his place behind the register.

"That's what I thought," Alfonso uttered, loud enough for Blake to hear.

"Asshole," Blake mumbled, soft enough that Alfonso couldn't.

After dealing with a wave of customers, Blake turned his back to the kitchen and sent a text to Greg.

Blake (9:17pm): I'm going to be later than expected. The fucking dick-head manager is making me stay til 11.

Greg (9:20pm): Just like that?

Blake (9:20pm): Just like that.

Greg (9:20pm): Prick

Blake (9:21pm): Yup

Greg (9:22pm): Come to the dorm when you're done. A bunch of us are gonna pregame for a while and then we'll go.

Blake (9:22pm): Go where?

Greg (9:23pm): Wherever the night takes us.

Blake (9:23pm): If I end up getting out too late, leave without me and I'll meet up with you if I can.

Greg (9:24pm): There are 24 hours in a day.

Blake (9:27pm): So...?

Greg (9:28pm): So it's never too late.

Blake (9:28pm): Are you already drunk?

Greg (9:30pm): I'm a little bit buzzy.

Blake (9:35pm): Cool. You'll be asleep in an hour.

Greg (9:36pm): Not true. I'll rally for you.

Blake (9:36pm): I'm honored.

Greg (9:37pm): As you should be.

Blake (9:37pm): See you soon.

Blake spent the next hour and a half giving excessive amounts of attention to every person who walked through the door. He figured the more he focused on them, the less he would focus on wanting to tell Alfonso off. By the time eleven rolled around, Blake didn't so much as a glance in the manager's direction before clocking out.

Putting his jacket on as he exited the building, he zipped it and wove through the Friday night crowds gathered outside the bars on State Street. A hint of winter mingled with the precipitation building in the October air and all Blake could think about was football, and how badly he wanted to go to a game. It had been so long since he'd been. Football was something he'd always done with his dad, and though his father was back in Lexington living with a gay couple, they only saw each other sporadically at best.

Deciding to go with his nostalgic urge, and well aware that his father would be up at that hour, Blake dialed his dad's number.

"Blake, man, how are you doing?" Jack asked in one breath the moment he answered the phone.

"Doing well. I just got off work and I'm walking to my friend's dorm to party. I figured I'd give you a call and see how things were?"

"Things are good. I'm moving and shaking as always. You know how I was living with Pete and Dave?"

"Was?" Blake questioned. "Past tense?"

"Past tense in a couple of weeks," Jack clarified. "I'm going to move in with Gemma. Remember Gemma?"

Blake hardly knew Gemma enough to remember her, but he answered, "Yeah," anyway.

"Things are good between us so we're going to give cohabitation a whirl. See how it goes."

"That's nice. I hope it works out."

"You know how these things are, they work until they don't and then they might work again, or they might not. Who knows?"

"Who knows," Blake agreed.

"How's your roommate situation going? Are you living with the same girl you were before?"

"Mm-hmm. She's on month-to-month on the apartment and has been talking about moving in with her girlfriend. So, we'll see. I can't afford it on my own, but I don't think she'd leave me high and dry."

"People will leave you high and dry if it means they're getting good and wet," Jack warned. "It's human nature, man. People look out for their own asses. That's why we have to work to elevate, you know? Come together and rise above our instinct to survive individually and focus on the opportunity to thrive as a community."

"Hmm," Blake hummed, not in the mood for one of his father's philosophical lectures.

"You should come over and have dinner with me, Pete and Dave. Maybe you could take my room when I make the move. You can check out my digs. They're great to live with and they wouldn't gouge you on price."

"I don't know if I'm looking right now. I'll have to talk to Bianca."

"Talk to her and then talk to me," Jack suggested. "I think it'd be cool for you to get to know them better."

"We'll see. It depends on what Bianca's going to do."

"Don't let other people dictate your direction in life."

"Alright. I'll call you soon," Blake said, as he walked into the lobby of Greg's dormitory.

"Later."

Blake took his identification card out of his wallet and presented it to the guard, embarrassed that he didn't have a license to show in its place. Ever since the crash junior year, he hadn't had a desire to get behind the wheel. As far as Blake was concerned, it wasn't a bad thing. It wasn't like he was able to afford a car anyway. What was the point of a license if you didn't have a vehicle to drive? His aversion was convenient, so he didn't fight it.

"Go on up," the uniformed man said, handing the card back to Blake, "but no funny business."

"I'm not funny at all," Blake promised, which he found kind of funny.

Unamused, the guard buzzed him in, watching as Blake got into the elevator and pushed the button for the fifth floor. Knowing he had an audience, Blake waved and leaned against the wall as the door drew closed.

He was excited to see Greg. Though they didn't get as much time together as Blake would have liked, they managed to see each other once a month. In an astonishing turn of events, Greg had decided to rush a fraternity, an action that both floored and concerned Blake. No matter how much his friend tried to deny it, Greg was sensitive as hell, and the thought of him dealing with the frat culture was worrisome. The last thing he wanted Greg to cope with was the toxic masculinity of hazing practices he'd heard dudes were made to participate in. Greg wasn't one to complain, but Blake wished he would've been more forthcoming about what kind of shit they put him through. Blake had met a few guys in Greg's pledge class, and although they seemed nice enough, he was skeptical.

Blake knocked on the door, grinning when his friend pulled it open and ushered him into the room. There were six guys squeezed into the small space, gathered around a glass bong as tall as their seated statures.

"How the fuck do you guys hide this thing?" Blake laughed. "It's the size of a chair."

"We have our ways," one of the guys smirked.

Settling in next to Greg, Blake listened to their stories of stealth while he took rips off the bong. When they were all good and baked, they decided to forgo the party and hit up a greasy spoon instead.

The restaurant Greg chose was a twenty-four-hour joint around the corner from the dorms. Though the interior was unimpressive, the atmosphere bubbled with the energy of youth. Tables and booths overflowed with students in various states of inebriation, their chatter and laughter filling the space as they shook off the responsibility of their week. Unlike White Knight Pizza, which only hosted the co-eds for a handful of minutes, the Tulip Tree Tavern was a place where people wanted to stay and extend their night, make more memories. Blake wished he worked at a restaurant that had a similar vibe, or a vibe at all. Every moment spent at the pizza shop was one he couldn't get back, but it seemed like the opposite for employees at the diner. They were integrated into the fold in a way he never would be at the shit shack he wasted his time at. It was nice to see people like him participating rather than blending into the walls. Blake had never been beige. It was hard to sink away.

As he enjoyed his cheeseburger, he considered the commute to the restaurant and internally debated whether he should ask for an application.

And then he did.

25

Blake's apartment was six miles from the Tulip Tree Tavern, but that didn't stop him from eagerly taking a fountain job when they offered it to him. Even the fact that he would be working third shift without the option of utilizing public transportation didn't give him pause. There was something about the place that felt right, which was a sensation Blake was driven to chase considering how wrong much had been for so long. Not only did Blake like the atmosphere, he found that he also appreciated the owner. Oliver was the polar opposite of Tony. While working at White Knight Pizza, Blake hardly interacted with his boss. Tony never stepped foot on the floor for any reason other than to get to the front door. In his two weeks at Tulip Tree Tavern, Oliver had worked every night. The volume of customers they served made it apparent to Blake that the restaurant was successful, but that didn't lessen Oliver's hard work. Though he had the ability to hire a night manager, he'd told Blake he preferred to take the hands-on approach, believing that his display of commitment would foster the same in his employees. As far as Blake was concerned, Oliver was right. Seeing the blood, sweat, and tears that the man on top was willing to put in made Blake want to work for him, want to learn from him.

Luckily, Oliver liked to teach and took Blake under his wing early on. Blake's first shift working at the Tulip Tree Tavern had been a nightmare. If anyone would have told him that scooping ice cream for milkshakes and filling glasses with soda would be stressful as hell, he never would have believed them. It wasn't as though the tasks were academically challenging or above his skill level, but goddamn if he hadn't found himself in the weeds. For every order he worked on, he had six more in queue. No matter how fast he tried to churn shit out, he was perpetually behind.

"You're alright," Oliver assured him. "Keep your head down. Knock out the orders and slide them across the counter, one after another, that's all you have to do, alright Blake? One after another. Head down, churn them out."

Blake nodded, trying to drown out the sound of the patrons' merriment and the waiters' demands. Work at the counter wasn't rocket science, but somehow, he felt the weight of the solar system on his shoulders. Realistically he knew it wasn't that heavy, but that didn't mitigate the stress. He wanted to do well, make Oliver proud, feel like he wasn't a fuck-up. There was too much emotion poured into the milkshakes and he was struggling to keep up, but it was good to give a shit about something, especially something within his immediate reach. For too long his goals had evaded his fingertips as he stretched to reach them, a slipping grip on things he should've held tight to. So instead, he wrapped his hands around glasses as he fulfilled orders, tangible markers of his success. One after another just like Oliver had said, and every treat delivered to a hungry mouth was an accomplishment. That didn't mean, however, that he didn't remain behind, even when he grew more comfortable with the job. The hubbub that drew him to the Tulip Tree Tavern was precisely what kicked his ass. If Blake dug deep enough he could uncover the life lesson there, but he didn't have time to sink into the soil, not when there were orders to fill.

The six-mile walk hadn't been too brutal until the weather went from cold to dangerous. Oliver thought that Blake was exaggerating when he called in on a January night and said he couldn't make it to work. As expected, Oliver had offered to pick him up. Blake had accepted. He didn't have any reason not to, especially when it was his boss who was making the suggestion.

As they worked on drinks, a news story broke about a man who had died because of the brutal temperatures.

"See that," Blake said, nodding toward the television to the left of the bar. "That could've been me. Fourteen degrees, man. That's freeze on contact shit."

"I thought you were being a pussy," Oliver confessed.

"I wasn't. Have you ever walked six miles in freezing temps?"

"You already know the answer to that question."

"There's always a moment when you think you won't make it, a split second where you think you've made a mistake that you can't take back. Your lungs get tight and your joints hurt."

"It's nothing I'd like to try," Oliver stated, pushing his floppy auburn hair out of his freckled face.

"It's better that way," Blake promised. "Believe me."

"I'll take your word for it."

"My word's good. I've wavered on a lot of things, but never on that."

"Then I'll trust you," Oliver grinned. "Have you thought about moving closer?"

"Have you thought about putting me on days?" Blake asked, garnering a sigh from Oliver.

"I don't have the space."

"I know," Blake said as he scooped a healthy helping of vanilla ice cream into a glass of root beer. "I have the opportunity to move closer."

"And..." Oliver prompted.

"And I just have to pull the trigger."

"Then by all means, do it."

"It's not like it's so much closer," Blake explained, thinking back to the dinner he'd had with Pete, Dave and his dad. "Four miles instead of six."

"I bet it feels significant when you're walking the final two," Oliver reasoned.

"No doubt."

Moving in with Peter and Dave was an attractive option. Not only was the house a few miles closer to work, it was as nice as the men who owned it. Rather than continue sleeping on an air mattress in a tiny room, Blake would have a king-size bed in a much more generous space. Only months before, his bedroom in Bianca's apartment had been the ultimate escape for him, a haven of privacy that he sorely lacked in rehab, the halfway house, and even at the Dempsey's. The concept of wanting something more after all he had been through was strange and as uncomfortable as the AeroBed had become. It was difficult for Blake to rationalize deserving better, but maybe he did, maybe there was a threshold of shit a person was supposed to endure, and he'd reached his. In the end, it was Bianca who pushed him toward the change. Her decision to move in with McKenna before Christmas had ensured that Blake was spending the New Year in his new home with a pair of awesome guys.

Peter and Dave were different from one another, but somehow, they had found a balance that gave them the strongest relationship Blake had ever witnessed. Admittedly, he'd never been around healthy long-term relationships, considering his parents had divorced during his toddler years and their subsequent unions with other people had been turbulent at best. The more time Blake spent with Peter and Dave, the more he realized that not only did he want to be in a relationship, but he wanted to be in one similar to theirs.

Though his Rise and Grind meet-ups had only led to a succession of one-night stands, Blake didn't abandon the app. It made connecting with guys too damn easy. Instead, he decided a change in his tactics was necessary. Ignoring the pictures that flaunted fit abs, Blake scanned the profiles for a handsome face. When he found a guy with kind brown eyes and rosy cheeks, he sent a message.

Blake: Hey. How's it going?
Jay: Well. How are you?
Blake: I'm doing well. I like your picture.

Jay: Really?

Blake: Yeah. What's not to like?

Jay: Thanks. You have a nice smile.

Blake: It's even better in person.

Jay: Maybe I'll see it someday.

Blake: How about tonight?

Jay: Tonight?

Blake: Yeah. I work at 10, but we could do something before that.

Jay: What do you do?

Blake: I make milkshakes at a diner.

Jay: How many people sing that "Milkshake" song to you?

Blake: Way too many to count.

Jay: I bet. I have a few friends over so we will probably have to do another night unless you want to come chill and smoke a bowl with us.

Blake: Where do you live?

Jay: Pine Bluff apartments on Waller and Broadway.

Blake: That's on my way to work. I can be there in an hour if that's cool.

Jay: That's definitely cool.

Blake: What's your apartment number?

Jay: 333

Blake: That's easy to remember. I'll see you soon.

Jay: Sounds good.

As Blake wrapped up in his winter gear, he couldn't help but be surprised. There were going to be other people at Jay's place. He hadn't asked him over with the intention of fucking. They were going to hang out, get to know each other, smoke some weed. It was unlike anything Blake had experienced on Rise and Grind before, and he found himself hoping that maybe it was the start of something different, something amazing.

26

As Blake climbed the stairs to Jay's apartment, he was impressed by the condition of the building. Though it was close to campus, it wasn't rundown by rowdy occupants. There were no beer cans or pizza boxes strewn on the grass of the common areas like he'd seen at various other complexes. It was clean and classy, which led Blake to believe that Jay would be the same. He wasn't disappointed.

"Hey," Jay greeted, opening the door. He shifted nervously as he moved aside to let Blake in. His nerves were palpable, which somehow set Blake at ease. He wouldn't be nervous if he hadn't liked what he'd seen. He wanted Jay to like what he saw. "Come in."

"Hey. Thanks," Blake said, glancing around the well-appointed living room. "Should I take off my shoes?"

Jay laughed a breathy laugh that had Blake wanting to do things that would elicit the sound again and again. "No, you can keep them on."

"Alright," Blake nodded. "Your place is really nice."

"Thanks. I like it," Jay said, leading Blake toward the couch where a guy was rolling joints as a girl messed around on her phone beside him. "Carly, Matt, this is Blake. Blake, Carly and Matt."

Blake shook their hands. "It's nice to meet you."

"You didn't shake mine," Jay stated, grinning when Blake reached out to make the connection.

Blake liked how Jay's smile and body were soft, and how their hands were the same size even though Jay had an inch on him. He liked that Jay was flirting and that his friends were going about their business. Blake liked it all.

"Now I did," Blake noted, giving Jay's hand an extra squeeze before letting go. It was nice to steal touches rather than steeling himself for the awkward moments after fucking another random guy in Rise and Grind.

Jay nodded and kneeled at the coffee table to help his friend roll. Squatting beside him, Blake watched Jay's nimble fingers, impressed by his technique. "Are you into smoking?"

Blake chuckled. "Yeah, I'm into smoking." Pulling his phone from his pocket, he checked the time. It was the first time since he'd gotten a job at the Tulip Tree Tavern that he wanted to call out, but regardless of how tempting it was to do so, he knew he had to show up to work. He had an hour before he needed to start walking to the diner. It didn't seem like enough time.

"How long can you stay?" he asked, eyeing Blake's phone.

"About an hour. If I don't start walking at nine I won't get to work in time."

"You walk to work?" Carly asked, crinkling her nose at the revelation. "How long does it take you?"

"From here it's an hour or so, but usually it's about two."

"Don't judge," Matt chided, elbowing her in her ribs gently.

"I'm not judging," Carly promised, tossing her thick blonde locks over her shoulder. "I'm curious. That's all."

"It's not a big deal," Blake said easily, noticing how Jay was regarding him with concern.

"I can drive you tonight," Jay offered. "That way you can hang out longer."

"You don't have to do that," Blake protested. "I'm used to walking."

"Well, I guess it depends on how long you want to stay here," Jay reasoned. "If you're not into it, then whatever. If you are...an hour is a lot more of a commitment than the five minutes it would take me to drive you to wherever it takes you an hour to walk."

"Why talk about him leaving when he's right here?" Matt huffed. "He's been around for a minute. Why count down the time?"

"I didn't mean to," Jay began, turning to Blake expectantly. "I'm not trying to rush you out."

Blake wanted to cup his hand around Jay's chin and tilt him into a kiss, but he refrained, remembering that they were in mixed company. He hardly knew the guy, but he was immediately drawn to his thoughtfulness. It was refreshing.

"It's fine," Blake assured. "I didn't think you were."

"Awkward," Carly muttered, still focused on her phone.

"Shh," Matt warned, earning him a scowl from his girlfriend.

"They're always like this," Jay informed Blake, handing him a joint and lighter. "You can get it started."

Placing the paper between his lips, Blake lit it up and took a deep inhale, allowing the smoke to inflate his lungs before it sputtered from his mouth. As they passed the joint, Blake learned about Jay and found he liked him more with every word that came out of his mouth.

Jay was smart and accomplished, two qualities that Blake hadn't realized were a huge turn-on prior to meeting the University of Kentucky sophomore. He was studying English and liked to reference books, but he did it in the least pretentious way possible, a way that made Blake want to read every one he mentioned. It was stimulating to have conversations that illuminated parts of Blake's brain which he hadn't enacted since he was in a classroom. Just talking to Jay was better than any sex Blake had had with dudes on Rise and Grind. He liked how different everything felt with Jay, how *he* felt with him. Although Blake didn't go into great detail about the shit he'd been through, he did tell Jay that he'd been expelled senior year and had earned his GED over the summer. Jay didn't flinch, which somehow gave Blake the validation he didn't know he was seeking.

When nine o' clock rolled around, Blake decided to be forthcoming with his intentions. "If you're cool with driving me to work I can stay for a while more."

The smile on Jay's face told Blake that was precisely what he wanted to hear. "I'm definitely cool with that."

"You should get us all some food while you're there," Matt suggested.

"I could go for some French fries," Carly agreed.

"No problem," Jay said, "Text me what you guys want when I leave, and I'll pick it up."

"He's always this amazing," Carly told Blake. "He's not fronting because you're here."

"Good to know," Blake nodded, grinning when he caught Jay's eyes.

As was typical when one was enjoying himself, the minutes flew by and before Blake knew it he was walking to the parking lot with Jay.

"That's yours?" Blake asked, pointing at the flashing taillights of a white Mercury Mountaineer.

"Yeah."

"Wow. It's nice," Blake said as climbed into the tan leather passenger seat. Though it had been obvious from the way Jay carried himself that he was successful, his car was further confirmation.

"Thanks," Jay replied, turning the key in the ignition.

The tension had grown unbearable for Blake, who gave into his urge to go for a kiss. "C'mere," he whispered, placing his hand on Jay's cheek. He closed the space between them, lips on lips as their tongues tangled and twisted together. The affection Blake felt for Jay increased with every rotation, so much so that he feared that if they continued kissing he'd be too far gone to actually drag his ass to work. Reluctantly, he pulled back, smiling at Jay as he did.

"You have to get to work," Jay sighed, looking as disappointed by that fact as Blake felt.

"Yup."

"The Tulip Tree Tavern, right?" He backed out of the parking spot. "I know where it is."

"Thanks for the ride," Blake said, buckling his seatbelt.

"It's no problem."

"It's nice, though, that you're leaving your friends to take me."

"I'm happy to," Jay promised. "What time do you get off?"

"Four."

"Give me a call and I'll pick you up."

Blake shook his head. "I'm not going to drag you out of bed to pick me up. I walk home every night. It's not a big deal."

"It's cold out," Jay stated. "I want to. I want to pick you up."

Blake was floored by the consideration and how genuine Jay was in his offer. "Okay. I'll call you. Thanks."

Jay nodded and parked the car in the lot outside the restaurant. "I'm going to come in and order their food and then I'll be back when you call me later."

"Sounds good," Blake said, stealing another kiss before they exited the car.

While Jay was waiting for his take-out order, Blake couldn't stop himself from sneaking peeks in his direction. He was handsome, and his kindness made him even sexier than Blake found him to begin with.

Jay smiled and waved at Blake before he left, and Blake kept his eyes fixed on him until he was no longer in view. He wanted to follow him, but he focused on getting through his shift and how he could get back to Jay's car as soon as it was done.

The night moved like molasses, and by the time he was ready to call Jay, Blake was exhausted, but still excited. It was odd to reach out to someone he barely knew to come give him a ride, but Jay had convinced him that he truly wanted to pick him up.

That was until he didn't answer the phone. Blake tried to call him twice before deciding that he should start walking. It was reasonable to assume that Jay was deep in sleep, so Blake did, even though the nagging whisper of negativity in his ear told him that maybe Jay thought better of it, that the act of care was too much too soon.

He was halfway home when his phone rang.

"Holy shit, I'm so sorry. I was dead asleep," Jay said as soon as Blake picked up.

"You don't have to apologize for sleeping at four in the morning," Blake laughed. "It's fine."

"Where are you?"

"I'm almost home. Don't worry about it."

"I told you I was going to come get you and I want to. Tell me where you are, and I'll be right there."

"It's not..."

"I keep my word," Jay interrupted. "Don't let me beat myself up for being a douchebag, alright?"

Grinning, Blake looked at the nearest street sign. "I'm at Maxwell and Madison."

"Be there in a few minutes. See you soon."

"You really don't have to..." Blake began, quickly realizing Jay was no longer on the line. "...come," he continued quietly, tucking his phone back into his pants pocket.

It was hard for Blake to believe that a catch like Jay was leaving his bed in the middle of the night just so Blake didn't have to walk home in the cold. It was even harder to believe that the shyer guy had smacked his lips against Blake's as soon as he climbed into his car, and that Blake could feel that much in a single moment. But it happened, and Blake was sure it would continue to happen a lot more.

27

L ying in bed wrapped up in Jay was exactly where Blake wanted to be, so that was where he was as often as possible. The more time they spent together, the less Blake wanted to be apart. Their relationship escalated quickly after the late-night-pickup-that-almost-wasn't, first emotionally and then physically. It was the second time someone Blake cared deeply about gave him their virginity, and he didn't take the privilege for granted. With his arms hooked over Jay's shoulders, he'd lost himself inside him, lips and hips locked as they rocked in unison. The weight of the moment should have felt heavy, but it was as light as Blake's heart. Everything was right.

"Do you like it?" Blake asked one morning as they peeled their sweaty bodies off of one another.

"I cum, don't I?" Jay replied, tracing his fingertip over the ridges of Blake's abdominal muscles. "Fuck, this body."

"What about it?"

"I like it."

"You like it?" Blake grinned, placing his hands behind his head and watching as Jay looked him over.

"I love it."

Lifting an eyebrow, Blake raked his fingers through his boyfriend's hair. "You love it?"

"I do," Jay confirmed, peppering his chest with kisses before inching up to slot their mouths together.

Blake kissed him eagerly, letting his hands travel up Jay's broad back. He tickled his pale skin gently as he inhaled his lover's soft sighs. Lifting his sleepy eyelids, Blake admired how the early morning sun seeped through the blinds and washed his man's face with a golden hue. "You're beautiful," he muttered, nuzzling his nose into the crook of Jay's neck, "so beautiful."

"Have you looked at yourself in the mirror lately?" Jay whispered, running the tip of his pointer finger down the slope of Blake's nose.

"Are we going to get into a debate over who's more gorgeous?" Blake laughed, reaching up to grasp Jay's hand firmly. He kissed his knuckles sweetly, savoring the scent of his skin. "I'm good at arguing, but I'd probably let you win."

"I wish I was as confident as you. That I had something to back it up with," Jay admitted, laughing when Blake gave him a hard smack on the bare ass.

"I love it when you back it up," Blake flirted, licking his lips as Jay shimmied his ass under his grasp. "Mmm, I like that."

"You do?" Jay hummed in a sing-song tone. "How much?"

"It's my favorite thing."

"Oh yeah? You like it better than video games?" Jay challenged, chuckling when Blake gave him several swift swats to the butt.

"You know what I like," Blake growled, smiling into the kiss Jay had laid on his lips. He liked him...a lot. "You drive me crazy, baby."

"Good. I want to, because then maybe you'll be half as gone as me."

"Half?"

"Half," Jay confirmed, snuggling into Blake's waiting arms.

"I'm there," Blake promised, twirling a lock of Jay's hair around his pinky.

"It's scary."

"What's scary?"

"Feeling these feelings so fast," Jay revealed, puckering his lips to ask for another kiss. Blake was happy to oblige. "Feeling these feelings at all maybe."

"I want you to feel them." *Because I feel them, too. Because I love you.* "Why?"

"Because I feel them, too," Blake confessed, debating whether he should continue his admission by letting the words on the tip of his tongue roll off or if he should swallow them down, holding them in his heart for a while longer.

As into him as Blake believed his boyfriend was, he knew Jay only managed to let go of his inhibitions in the tender moments before yanking himself back to a place of fear. While it was frustrating for Blake to deal with his boyfriend's second-guessing, he knew he had to be patient. Coming to terms with his sexuality had been a process for Jay, and the fact that he wasn't ready to tell his family he was gay made things more difficult. Regardless of how often Jay assured Blake he was all in, Blake could tell the secrecy impeded his boyfriend's ability to confidently move forward in their relationship. Despite his foresight and belief that things would be better for Jay when he shared his truth, Blake never pushed. Impatience was the enemy of growth and he didn't want to stunt Jay's progress with his haste. Still, he wished Jay would stop standing in his own way.

"You do?" Jay questioned, humming quietly when Blake intertwined their fingers.

"You know I do."

"I like to hear it."

"That's good because I like to tell you," Blake grinned.

"So tell me," Jay prompted. Though his tone was innocent, Blake could hear the challenge in the sentiment, for Blake to say it and for Jay to accept.

"You want me to?" Blake whispered, a subtle melody dancing playfully in his voice. "Tell you how I feel about you? You want that?"

"Yes."

"I love you," Blake said matter-of-factly, because the statement was unequivocally true. He loved how even just being in Jay's presence made him want to be better, how Jay assured him that success wasn't measured by assets while Blake worked to keep his life on track. How supportive he was of where Blake came from and where he was headed. He loved the way Jay loved him, even though his boyfriend had never spoken the words. His actions were resounding.

Though Blake had been fairly confident in what Jay was hinting toward in his campaign for clarity, he doubted it in the moment of silence that followed his admission. As the seconds passed, Blake grew more unsure of himself until Jay finally replied, "I love you, too."

"Yeah?" Blake grinned, his heart swelling in his chest at the sound of the phrase coming from his boyfriend's mouth. He didn't know how much he needed to hear it until he did.

Snaking his hand behind Jay's head, Blake drew him closer, hungrily slotting their lips together for a kiss that was rife with emotion and happiness. Things between them were instantly more solid and serious than they had been before the utterances, and it was all so right.

"Now I don't want to go to class," Jay groaned, as he broke away from the kiss. "I want to stay here with you all day."

"You say that whenever we're in bed like this," Blake smirked.

"You're temptation personified," Jay flirted, grabbing Blake by the waist and pulling him in closer.

"Mmm," Blake moaned as his boyfriend sucked gently on the dip of his neck. "I love it when you talk literary to me."

Jay laughed lightly, the warmth of his breath fanning over Blake's skin, tickling him as his lips tingled, needy for more kisses. "I love that you love it."

"There's a whole lot of love going on right now," Blake chuckled, smacking Jay's ass hard enough to get him to lift his head. "I don't want you to, but you have to go, babe. You're gonna be late."

"Why do you have to be so responsible?" Jay joked, standing up to stretch his arms over his head before he grabbed a towel from his closet.

"That's the first time anybody's ever complained about my level of responsibly being on the 'too responsible' end."

"I'm not sure what that says about me."

"Honestly, I'm not either," Blake chuckled tapping his fingers against his torso as he admired Jay's body. "You look good standing over there in your towel."

"Fuck off," Jay smirked, tightening the knot around his hips.

"You do," Blake said, sitting up and waggling his eyebrows. "I'm about to ruin my new-found responsibility streak and tell you to get your ass back over here."

"You wouldn't want to ruin a one-day streak, would you? C'mon," Jay chided playfully as he licked his lips.

He appeared to be considering something, and Blake knew the responsible thing to do would be to tell his boyfriend to get in the shower, but responsibility was a real cockblocker when his man looked as good as he did. Jay's body was a marvel of strength and softness. Though it wasn't conventionally considered to be the archetypal male form, it was perfect for Blake because it belonged to Jay, because of how the flesh felt when he clawed it in the throes of passion, because it was where the person he loved lived.

"I'd ruin it if you let me," Blake decided, smiling as Jay dropped the towel and crawled toward him on the bed. "You're not supposed to let me," he laughed as Jay kissed his way down his body.

"In this situation it works out in my favor," Jay grinned, continuing his descent. "So, I'm going to just go with it."

"At my expense?" Blake tsked, loving every minute of his boyfriend's rebellion.

"We all have to make sacrifices."

"I want it on record that I told you to go to class," Blake said, sighing as Jay took him into his mouth, "but you can add an addendum that I'm glad you didn't."

"Noted," Jay mumbled around Blake's dick.

Responsibility was overrated.

28

Jay was too generous to Blake. He gave him endless kisses, tons of attention, and the keys to his car—which turned out to be a massive mistake. While driving Jay's Mountaineer, Blake always attempted to be overly cautious, not only because his boyfriend's car was nice as hell, but also due to his pesky little lack of a license. He'd been forthcoming about his unlawful status with Jay, and his man had said annoyingly perfect shit like, "I trust you" and "I know you're careful," statements which made Blake feel even worse about the fender bender.

He knew he was fucked the moment it happened. Maybe that's why he reacted the way he had. The stress of the circumstance had made him momentarily insane enough to flip off the school teacher he'd rear-ended when she tried to take him to task. The amount of trouble he'd been in in his life had conditioned Blake to posture in such situations, refusing to show a semblance of weakness. In hindsight, the better approach would have been contrition. If he'd kissed the lady's ass a bit perhaps he would have been able to apologize and move on, avoiding the subsequent call to the police and the revelation that he wasn't road ready. Blake cursed his temper as he stood on the side of the road trying to figure out how to explain the accident to his boyfriend. Knowing Jay, he would let Blake off the hook even though he should've held him accountable.

"The car's whatever," Jay said as he surveyed the minimal damage to the front bumper, "It shouldn't take much to buff it out. I'm more worried about what I'm going to tell my parents."

"Why would you have to tell them anything?"

Jay narrowed his eyes at Blake, who narrowed his back. "Because it's their car. It's not like they won't find out when they start getting shit in the mail and their insurance premiums go up."

"Wait, your parents own the car?"

"Yeah. I don't have a job, Blake," Jay reminded him as if he was an imbecile. "How would I own a car?"

"They could've bought it for you or something," Blake reasoned, a familiar pressure of anxiety settling on his chest. "Fuck. What are you going to tell them?"

"Right. That's what I'm trying to figure out. There's no way they'd believe I'd let a friend drive it," Jay said, sitting down on the curb, "especially a friend who doesn't have a license."

"Tell them that I had a really important doctor's appointment, or a job interview, and you were doing me a big favor," Blake offered, taking a seat beside his boyfriend. "I mean, you're a nice guy, they'd believe you were doing someone a favor, wouldn't they?"

"No. The only thing that could make me stupid enough to let an unlicensed driver take my car is love, or at the very least sex," Jay sighed, rubbing his forehead as if he was trying to stimulate his brain to give him a possible excuse.

"I'm sorry," Blake uttered, feeling more so by minute. The last thing he wanted to do was complicate Jay's life in any way, but it seemed the little accident was going to cause a huge wreck for his boyfriend.

"I should tell them the truth," Jay decided, both knees bouncing as he stared forward at the car. "I should just tell them the truth. I'm gay, right? I should tell them that. I should tell them that I'm gay and that I'm in a relationship with you, and that I let you drive the car because you don't have one. That we share things, you know, the way people in relationships do, because we're in a relationship...a gay one," he rambled.

Blake considered interrupting the outpouring of repetitive statements but thought better of it. Jay was processing what would be one of the most important conversations he would have in his life and Blake didn't want to cut short any of his thoughts about the matter.

"Because I'm gay," Jay continued, "and they should know that. We're serious about each other..." he looked to Blake for confirmation.

"Of course we are," Blake promised, placing his hand on Jay's knee, trying to calm its bobbing.

"They should know that."

"Okay," Blake nodded. "Whatever you think is right." He paused for a moment, debating whether he should bring his concerns to light. Unable to hold himself back, he noted, "They're probably not going to be so crazy about me after all this though. I should've never driven your car without a license. They'll be pissed, and they won't think I'm good for you."

"I think they'll be more shocked by my sexuality than the fact that I let you drive my car. I think the whole car thing will pale in comparison to the bigger admission."

"I don't want you to come out to take the heat off the accident," Blake protested.

"It's not like that," Jay huffed. "It's just the impetus I guess." He pulled his phone out of his pocket. "I should call them now."

"Here on the side of the road? Why don't you wait until we get back to your place? It will be quieter, and you can have some privacy."

"Who's around?" Jay asked, presenting the empty shoulder to Blake.

"Me."

"I want you here."

"Okay, then I'm here," Blake promised.

He watched as Jay's hands shook while he dialed his parents' number. When he brought the phone to his ear, Blake held his free hand, attempting to steady it, to steady him.

"I can't believe I'm doing this," he muttered as he waited for them to pick up.

"It's alright," Blake assured. "It will be alright."

From what Jay had told Blake about his parents, they were good people who loved their son. While Blake didn't foresee the revelation of Jay's sexuality being a huge issue for them, he also didn't understand why it was a big deal to anybody.

"Mom," Jay said into the phone. "Is dad there?" he paused. "Yeah, I need to talk to you both."

Blake's heart pounded as he waited for Jay to open his mouth again.

"Should I put them on speaker?" Jay whispered. "So you can hear how it goes?"

Blake cringed, not sure what to say. "That's up to you. However you want to handle it."

"I'll put them on speaker," Jay decided. "That way if I black out or something you can tell me what we said."

"Black out?" Blake cried, clamping his lips shut as soon as he heard a male voice come over the line.

"Jay?"

"Hey, dad."

"Is everything okay?"

"Yeah. Mom are you on, too?"

"Yes. You're making us nervous," Mrs. Dennison said. The stress in her tone would have made the fact apparent without the explicit acknowledgment.

"It's not..." Jay began, clearing his throat, "It's not really a big deal."

"Well then out with it," Mr. Dennison urged. "The buildup is brutal."

"The Mountaineer was in a little accident."

"Oh my goodness. Are you hurt?" Mrs. Dennison asked, her voice rising an octave.

"No. I'm not."

"Did you hit somebody, or did someone hit you? Was insurance information exchanged? Were the police called?" Mr. Dennison questioned.

"I wasn't actually in the car," Jay admitted.

"You weren't actually in the car," Mr. Dennison repeated. "What do you mean you weren't actually in the car? Who was driving?"

Jay cleared his throat again as Blake held his breath, knowing the moment was upon them. "My boyfriend was driving."

"Your boyfriend was driving," Mr. Dennison said slowly.

"His *boyfriend* was driving," Mrs. Dennison told her husband. "So, what Jay's saying is that he has a boyfriend, and it was his boyfriend who was in the accident."

"Right," Jay confirmed.

"Okay," Mr. Dennison exhaled, "and is your boyfriend hurt?"

"Um, no, he's alright. It was a fender bender. The only damage is some denting on the other car and some scrapes on ours."

"Tell them I'll pay for the damages," Blake whispered, aware that the commitment would mean picking up additional shifts at work.

"He'll pay for the damages, but there's something else," Jay confessed, cringing at Blake, who cringed right back at him. "He doesn't have a license so I'm not sure how that will impact our insurance policy."

"Jay!" Mr. Dennison scolded. "Why was he driving if he doesn't have a license? That's completely asinine and irresponsible!"

"Dan," Mrs. Dennison cautioned. "Jay just *came out* and told us everything, so while it was a mistake that he allowed this boy to drive the car, it's important to remember that he could have been secretive but that he's *coming out* and telling us."

"I'm not worried about the gay thing, Jane," Jay's father sighed. "I'm worried about the fact that my son seems to have his head up his butt and isn't making good decisions."

"It was a mistake. I know it was a mistake. Blake knows it's a mistake. I'm sorry. Nothing like this will ever happen again," Jay promised.

"Blake," Mrs. Dennison noted. "That's your boyfriend's name? Blake? When do we get to meet him?"

Blake couldn't help but smile at Mrs. Dennison's complete disregard of what had occurred, and hyper-focus on her son's relationship.

"I'll talk to him about it," Jay replied, looking like the weight of the world had been removed from his shoulders.

"I'm going to need to speak with you and Blake about the financial ramifications for this accident once I figure out what I'm dealing with," Mr. Dennison states. "I'm not saying that's all we'll talk about, but I want to get this settled before I can think about anything else."

"I understand," Jay said, grinning when Blake squeezed his hand.

It wasn't the ideal circumstance, but as they got into the Mountaineer, with Blake sitting comfortably in the only seat he planned to sit in for as long as he didn't have his license, he could see the realization in Jay's eyes that everything was okay and that, maybe now, it would be even better.

And that's what he wanted for him.

29

Going to Louisville to meet Jay's parents two weeks after the fender bender wasn't necessarily on Blake's short list of shit he wanted to do, but he went anyway. It was important to Jay, and Jay was important to him. Ever since Blake had earned Claire's parents' immediate disapproval, the concept of "meeting the parents" was nerve-wracking. The added stress of the Dennisons being privy to one of his latest infractions didn't make things any easier on Blake.

"I'm kind of nervous," Blake admitted as they got out of the Mountaineer.

The neighborhood was nice, with tree-lined streets and well-manicured lawns. The pride of ownership was apparent, and Jay's tidiness was undoubtedly an outcome of the environment. It wasn't as though Blake came from squalor, but the suburban lifestyle felt different than the rural roads he'd grown up on. Although he had seamlessly transitioned into city living, he still struggled to shake the country from his bones. Wide spaces had given way to an array of places and Blake wondered if he would feel settled anywhere.

"I am, too," Jay stated, much to Blake's chagrin.

Blake stopped dead in his tracks, so he could show Jay he was pressed. "You're supposed to say things to make me feel better about this, you being nervous doesn't make me feel better."

"Do you want me to lie to you?" Jay asked. "I mean, I love you and I hope they will, too."

"You don't think they will?"

"I didn't say that."

"But you're sort of alluding to it," Blake said. "Don't you think? By saying you love me and you hope they will, I think it implies doubt."

"Am I not supposed to doubt it?" Jay questioned, appearing to be as confused as Blake felt. "I've never done this before, brought anyone home, now I am...and it's you."

"What's wrong with me?"

"Nothing's wrong with you. You're a guy. That's all I'm saying. I didn't break them in with a girl. I went from zero to sixty."

"Do you really think they needed to be 'broken in'?" Blake scoffed. "Wouldn't that have complicated things? They would've thought you were a certain way and expected it, not realizing that you weren't that way at all."

"That's too much for me think about right now," Jay tsked. "I know they'll like you. There's nothing not to like."

Blake wholeheartedly disagreed, but there was no reason to get into his detriments when Jay already knew what they were and chose not to acknowledge them. "There are a ton of things not to like."

"I disagree."

"Your parents wouldn't," Blake retorted.

"You don't have to tell them everything."

"That makes me feel like you're ashamed of my past."

"Of course I'm not."

"You could've fooled me," Blake scoffed, crossing his arms over his chest. Sometimes it was easier to lash out than to take a deep breath and calm himself down.

"Now you're just trying to pick a fight," Jay rolled his eyes. "I don't know why. Maybe you're overwhelmed."

"That's a good guess considering I'm standing outside your parents' house a few weeks after I crashed their car without a license.

This isn't, like, low-level grievances. I managed to majorly fuck shit up from the jump."

"You're thinking about the bad stuff too much."

"I could say you're not thinking about it enough," Blake shot back.

"You could but you'd be wrong. They've been good about things, but it's different when something's an idea versus when it's actually right in front of your face." Jay held his hand up in front of Blake's face for affect and grinned when Blake grabbed it and planted a series of smooches on his palm. "We're about to be right in front of their faces. Believe me, I've thought about it all but I'm trying to focus on the positive."

"That's very Zen of you."

"I'm probably going to shit my pants when we walk through the door," Jay deadpanned. "So, there's that."

"Don't do that," Blake laughed. "You'll ruin dinner."

"C'mon," Jay urged, lacing their fingers together as he guided Blake toward the porch.

Blake was surprised that Jay was holding his hand in such close proximity to the Dennisons' house and wondered if he was going to show the affection in front of his parents. His question was answered when Jay broke the connection to twist the doorknob and didn't initiate it again as they stood in the foyer.

Blake's palms began to sweat as he heard footsteps approaching. Nonchalantly, he wiped his hands on the thighs of his jeans before tucking them into his pockets. He wanted to look calm, but he was sure he was failing miserably.

Jay's parents looked like Blake had expected them to. Good southern Christians complete with their crosses and matching polo shirts. He could immediately feel Mrs. Dennison's warmth and a chill from her husband, who didn't seem glad to see Blake in the least. Though he was unsure whether Mr. Dennison's disposition was due to the fact Blake was Jay's boyfriend or because he'd messed up his car, he didn't feel particularly embraced, even after Jay's mom hugged her son and moved on to give Blake a nice tight one.

"It's so nice to meet you, Blake," she crooned. "Aren't you handsome!"

"Thank you, ma'am. It's great to meet you too," he replied, sneaking a glance at Mr. Dennison's unimpressed glare.

"If it isn't the car-wrecker himself," Mr. Dennison snarked, extending his hand after earning a look from his wife.

"Uh, hello, Sir. I am really sorry about that and I fully intend to pay you back every penny."

"Oh, you better believe I'm going to hold you to that."

"I expect that you won't be as reckless with my son as you are with our vehicle?" Mr. Dennison continued.

"He's just giving you a hard time," Mrs. Dennison said with a click of her tongue. "Stop it, Dan. Let's go sit down and get to know each other," she suggested, leading them to the living room.

Blake had barely sat down when Mr. Dennison asked, "Speaking of hard time, have you done any?"

"Dad," Jay cried. "Come on."

Blake cleared his throat, trying to loosen the stress that had settled there. "No. It's fine, of course not."

"Of course? Driving without a license is illegal. Why would it be 'of course'? Are we to assume that's the only illegal activity you've embarked on?"

"Dan," Mrs. Dennison warned as Jay shook his head.

"I'm going to go..." Blake gestured toward the general direction where he imagined the bathroom would be.

"Down the hall, second door to the right," Jay told him.

As soon as Blake was safely in the bathroom, he slid down the wall and tried to catch his breath. He was overreacting. He knew he was overreacting, but that didn't stop him from overreacting. He needed to get it together. Fast. Knowing exactly who could calm him down, he pulled out his phone.

Blake (4:36pm): Hey
Greg (4:37pm): Hey. How's it going with the rents?
Blake (4:37pm): I'm hiding in the bathroom.
Greg (4:37pm) So better than expected then?

Blake (4:37pm) Ha

Greg (4:38pm): I'm glad you still think I'm funny.

Blake (4:38pm): That was a sarcastic ha.

Greg (4:38pm) Yeah I got that, bathroom boy. Get back out there.

Blake (4:39pm): His dad's joking around about the car but I can tell he's kinda serious and I'm sweating.

Greg (4:39pm): Splash your face with cold water and chill the fuck out. You're a charming bastard. Be yourself. They'll love you.

Blake (4:40pm): Alright. Thanks.

Blake did as he was told, letting the water drip down his face for a moment as he attempted to gather the strength to go back out to the living room. The mood had shifted, and Blake suspected Mr. Dennison had gotten a talking-to from his wife.

"So, have your parents met Jay?" Mrs. Dennison asked when Blake sat down beside Jay on the couch.

"Um, my dad has. He lives in Lexington, but my mom hasn't come up to the city in a few months. She's in Unionville."

"That's not far. You guys haven't gone out there?" she asked with a click of her tongue. "Does she know you're gay? About Jay?"

"She definitely knows about Jay," Blake said, choosing not to correct her assumption about his sexuality. "I kind of avoid going to Unionville."

"For any particular reason?" Mr. Dennison asked skeptically. He probably thought Blake had warrants out for him in the county.

"Don't pry," Mrs. Dennison chided.

"It's nothing specific," Blake said. "It's just...I like having my mom in Lexington more. We try new restaurants and stuff."

"That's nice!" she exclaimed. "I'd love to come to Lexington and eat at good restaurants."

"You're welcome any time, Mom. I told you that," Jay said, wrapping his arm around his mother's shoulder.

"Well, for now we'll all have to settle for my cooking," Mrs. Dennison grinned. "Are y'all hungry?"

"Absolutely," Blake nodded, even though his stomach was busy churning with nerves.

"I could eat," Jay agreed.

"Jane fixed pot roast and her world-famous macaroni and cheese. Did Jay tell you about it, Blake?" Mr. Dennison asked.

"In fact, he did. He brings it up every time we make the boxed stuff. I'm excited to try it.

"Is that right?" Mrs. Dennison beamed. "I made enough to send you guys back with some leftovers to stock your freezer."

"Awesome," Jay said with a smile.

Blake could see the levity in his boyfriend's face, and as they all settled into an easy conversation over dinner, Blake smiled, too.

30

The day had started off like any other. Jay went to school while Blake slept. They played video games all afternoon, and then ate dinner before Blake got ready for work. The night, however, was different. It was unseasonably cold for late-March with huge grey clouds hanging heavy in the indigo sky, their bellies full of precipitation that, oddly enough, may have been snow. Jay was cold, too, more quiet than usual as he drove Blake to work. Figuring his boyfriend had a lot on his mind in regards to school, Blake remained silent, staring out the window at the pedestrians walking the sidewalks of Main Street. Instinctively, he placed his hand on Jay's leg, the lack of conversation causing him to feel disconnected. Though Blake had savored moments to himself in the past, the more time he spent with Jay, the less he wanted solitude. Sitting in the car beside his boyfriend, Blake felt an overwhelming feeling of loneliness, an emotion he had a difficult time inserting the impetus for. It was as if his mind understood what his heart didn't want to believe.

The way Jay shifted the car into park felt final, like it was the last time he'd ever pull into a space outside the Tulip Tree Tavern and watch Blake walk into the restaurant. The air had shifted, the inevitable still unspoken between them. Blake wanted to keep it that way. He wanted to get out of the car and avoid the conversation he feared. He wanted to be wrong, but he wasn't.

"We can't do this anymore," Jay whispered. "I can't do this."

"Do what?" Blake asked. "Be in a healthy loving relationship with a guy who's crazy about you? You can't do that anymore?"

Jay sighed and dropped his face into his hands. "I don't know how to explain it."

"Please try, because I don't get it. I thought things were going really great. I'm paying your dad back as fast as I can."

"It's not that," Jay said, quickly. "Not at all. You're pulling me away from my studies."

"How am I doing that?" Blake asked defensively. "I always tell you to go to class."

"The only real time we can spend together is in the afternoon when I should be studying. It makes me not want to go to class and stay in with you. You're distracting me from my goals."

There wasn't much to say to that besides "fuck," so that's exactly what Blake muttered. He'd had a hard-enough time trying to achieve his goals, he didn't want to hold Jay back from doing what he'd set out to do. It didn't hurt any less, though. He wanted Jay to succeed but he imagined he would be by his side when he did. Once they'd gotten past the fender bender and Jay's coming out, Blake thought the challenging stuff would be behind them, but evidently he was wrong. "I guess I'll go," he said slowly, hoping Jay would tell him not to. When he didn't, Blake got out of the car, not looking back when he heard Jay drive away.

One of the qualities Blake found the most attractive in Jay was his determination, so he had to acknowledge the college student's consistency, despite how badly it sucked to be sacrificed for his ambition. He didn't want to stand in his way, but he didn't think he had. If he hadn't known Jay better, Blake would have suspected that he met someone else, but he knew that wasn't the case. It felt worse. As if none of what meant something to Blake had been anything to Jay. There was no one to entice him away, he'd left on his own. Jay had wanted what was best for himself and it wasn't Blake. That type of rejection was difficult to cope with.

Walking into the Tulip Tree Tavern, Blake was numb. It looked to be business as usual in the restaurant, but things seemed to be moving slower than they typically did, at least through Blake's eyes. He needed to get behind the counter and immerse himself in the hustle and bustle of milkshake-making. Once the orders started rolling in, he wouldn't be able to think of anything but his aching wrist and the ice cream he had to scoop next.

"Do you feel okay?" Oliver asked, placing his hand on Blake's back as he leaned over the freezer. "I noticed you looked a little pale when you got here, out of it or something."

"Yeah, I'm fine," Blake answered, standing up to acknowledge his boss. "Remember how we talked about me picking up more shifts?"

"Yup."

"I'd like even more if it's possible." He wanted to pay off Mr. Dennison as expeditiously as he could.

"You're not going to have much of a social life if that's the case. I'm all about hard work, but it's important to have a balance."

"I'll be alright."

"Then I'll have you come in every night next week," Oliver decided.

"And if any days become available?"

"Then I'll keep you in mind."

Blake nodded, figuring he may as well distract himself with work. After all, it was more productive than drinking, which is precisely what he was compelled to do. He needed to keep it together, to stay on track. He'd had setbacks and heartbreaks before. He wasn't going to throw away all of his progress in dealing negatively with another one. Shit happened. *Bad* shit happened, but he wasn't going to let his life go to shit because of it, not anymore. He'd come too far, and he had further yet to go.

The trek home was awful, not only because his body was tired, but because Jay hadn't been waiting in the lot for him after work as he had each night after their first. Blake couldn't help but wonder why it was important to Jay to help him out when he hardly knew him, but easy for him not to show once he truly did. It was a mind-fuck, just like everything that had happened earlier that evening.

Half of him hoped he'd see Jay's car, that his ex-boyfriend would realize he'd made a mistake and follow his route to pick him up, but Jay seemed to think his only mistake was being with Blake in the first place. He should've known it wouldn't work out between them. Jay was everything Blake thought he would be until his sophomore year of high school. He was a college guy who focused on his studies and hung out with his friends in his nice apartment. It was unreasonable for Blake to believe he could have been a part of the life that got away. For months he'd fooled himself into thinking he could have what he'd long since given up. Maybe it was time he resigned himself to the fact again, he remembered where he stood thanks to how far he'd fallen in the past.

It had been a while since he went back home after work, but there was something comforting about Dave's presence in the kitchen when he entered the house. Like him, Dave worked third shift at a restaurant, and it was nice to not feel like he was the only person awake in the world.

"Peanut butter and jelly?" the older man offered, holding his plate out so Blake could take half of the sandwich.

"Thanks," he said as he took a bite. "How was work?"

"It was work," Dave grinned, sipping his water. "I'm assuming it was work for you as well."

"It was, in fact, work," Blake confirmed.

"I know technically you live here, but it's been a while since you've been here."

"Mm-hmm."

Dave raised his eyebrows. "Are you and Jay fighting?"

It was rare for them to have conversations about anything beyond sports, but Blake's mere presence was an admission that there was a problem.

"He broke up with me."

"Wow," Dave grimaced as if the news had physically struck him. "Were you expecting it, or did it take you by surprise?"

"I think I'm still in shock."

"What did he say? Did he give you any indication of what it was that went wrong?"

"He said I was a distraction or something. I don't know. I tell him to go to class, and he usually does, but I wasn't about to kick him out of his own place while he's sucking my dick," Blake laughed wryly. "If I'd known it would cause this to happen I would have."

"That would take some major self-control."

"Yeah, well, I can have some of that when I need to." He'd kicked an Adderall habit, he was sure he could have kicked the elicit-class-skipping blowjobs if he had to. "I guess what's done is done."

"You don't think he'll come around after the semester is over?"

Blake hadn't considered the chance. "Do you think he will?"

"I don't know him well, but if that was really the issue I don't see why he wouldn't want to rekindle things."

"Hmm."

"Would you go back with him if that happened?"

"It's a pretty shitty feeling to be dropped, but I've started things up with people who'd dumped me before. Who knows? I mean, I love him."

"Love's a strong word."

"It's an even stronger feeling," Blake noted, popping the last bite into his mouth. "Thanks for the sandwich," he murmured. "I'm going to go to bed."

"Don't waste time getting back into the game. You know what they say, 'The best way to get over someone is to get under someone new.'"

"I'll keep that in mind," Blake said.

Hooking up with a random person was the last thing he wanted to do. The first thing was rewind time.

31

Two weeks had softened Blake's hard stance not to get on Rise and Grind for a hookup. There had been no communication between him and Jay, and as much as he wished things could have been different, they weren't. The more he thought about the breakup, the less he understood Jay's motives. If it was really about his schoolwork, Jay could have easily said that they needed to spend less time together, and Blake would have gone along with it. Ending something amazing was too extreme to comprehend, yet it had happened, so there was no use dwelling on it any more than he already had. As much as he hoped Jay would come around, was as much as he doubted he would. Jay had a plethora of positive qualities, but as far as Blake was concerned, his stubbornness wasn't one of them. While they hadn't butted heads often, their shared propensity to hold their ground made for some lively discussions. It was unlikely Jay would go back on a decision he'd made, even if it was as complicated as a matter of the heart.

Blake decided that devoting himself to celibacy while waiting for Jay to come around would be a level of self-flagellation worse than his crime of being "too tempting." He'd move on and tempt someone who wanted to be tempted by him, and he wouldn't feel like he was complicating their lives when they made the decision to be with him. Though he wasn't looking for anything serious, he wanted to feel like he was adding something to someone's life, not fucking it up. Blake knew he was sensitive about subjects surrounding "the future," but he was tired of apologizing for the scars of his past.

Within moments of reactivating his Rise and Grind account, Blake had a message from a guy named Tom, who had the typical profile of his bare torso. He was in nice shape, but the picture didn't draw him in the way Jay's headshot had. Chiding himself for the comparison, Blake replied to the generic "hey."

Blake: Hey. How's it going?

Tom: Good. You?

Blake: Well.

Tom: What are you up to?

Blake: About to head to work.

Tom: This late?

Blake: Yeah I work nights at a diner.

Tom: Brutal

Blake: It's not too bad.

Tom: I'm hitting up State with some friends. You should meet up when you're done.

Blake: The bars will be closed.

Tom: According to the age on your profile you couldn't get in anyway!

Blake: I have my ways.

Tom: Oh yeah?

Tom: What time are you off?

Blake: Three

Tom: We'll still be going. Hit me up if you want to come over. I live on Columbia a half a mile north of Rose. We have a handle of strawberry vodka to get through. We could use an extra mouth.

Blake: An extra mouth, huh? Alright.

Tom: 7243 Columbia Ave

Blake knew going to some dude's place to *start* drinking at nearly four in the morning wasn't a great idea, but he'd been so uptight about the breakup, he needed an out-of-the-ordinary experience to loosen him up. Even if he ended up not liking Tom, he would like the free alcohol and the short walk to get it.

The townhouse was in a state of disrepair that Blake expected when college kids were the tenants, which only reminded him of Jay's apartment and how it wasn't like that. How Jay was different. Pushing his glasses up to press the heels of his hands against his eyes, he willed himself to mentally move on, at least for the night. When Tom answered the door, Blake was glad to see he was cute. He had a couple of inches on Blake and a lithe body that looked good in his well-fitted long sleeve shirt. There was no doubt Tom could lead Blake on a journey out of his head and into his bed.

"Damn," Tom grinned, obviously inebriated thanks to his evening activities. "You're fucking hot as hell."

Blake licked the smile off his lips and ran his hands through his hair. "You're pretty hot, too."

"Come in," Tom prompted, guiding Blake into the house.

The interior was nicer than the exterior, with an attempt at decorating apparent. Though the hot pink and zebra threw him off a bit, Blake could appreciate the creativity.

"I live with girls," Tom explained, as if he'd read Blake's expression and deduced he was confused by the explosion of tackiness.

"I see that," Blake said, noticing the sexy brunette sitting among the mountain of throw pillows on one of the couches.

"Annie," she said, glancing up from her phone for long enough to realize she wanted to put it down on the coffee table and pay attention to Blake. "And you are?"

"Blake," he replied.

"Our new drinking buddy that I met on Rise and Grind." Tom enunciated the name of the app as an explicit cue for Annie to stand down.

"Ah," she nodded. "Too bad."

"I'm bi," Blake added, garnering a glare from Tom. "Just saying."

"Got it," Annie smirked, giving Tom the finger. "Let's get to it then." She twisted the top off the store-brand vodka bottle and over-poured three shots.

"She has a healthy hand," Tom joked, holding up his glass. "To new friends."

"To new friends."

The cheers were the first of many, each proclamation becoming messier as the contents of the handle dwindled. By the time it was empty, Blake was more loaded than he'd ever been, and though the sweetness of the flavored liquor and lemonade had him queasy, he managed to find himself in a major make-out session with an obliterated Tom. It was sloppy but hot, and even though Blake couldn't recall falling asleep, he definitely remembered waking up.

"You won't believe how much money we just made!" a female shrieked. The volume of her voice drilled into Blake's eardrums and down through his teeth. He was pissed by the jarring wakeup call until he opened his eyes to find Annie and two other gorgeous girls standing topless at the foot of Tom's bed. Evidently the best way to get over an impending hangover was to be woken up by three sets of nice tits. Blake reached for his glasses to enhance the view.

"How much did you make?" Tom asked, yawning as he propped himself up on his elbows.

"Three thousand," Annie smiled. "Not bad for two hours."

"Holy shit," Blake gasped. "What do you guys do? Are you strippers or something?" He hummed, wishing he'd bit his tongue before making the assumption.

"No. We're cam girls," the third woman corrected. "We take off our clothes on camera and people send us money."

"So, virtual strippers," Blake stated, his mind going a mile a minute. "That's all you do? Take off your clothes?"

"Sometimes we use dildos, masturbate, do shows together. It just depends on what we're into at the time."

"And how much we want to make," Annie added.

"Wow. It would take me, like," Blake paused to figure it out, "two months to make that kind of money."

"Two hours," the first girl smirked. "And you can do it whenever you want. There are always people online ready to spend that green. Anyway, we're going to Waffle House if you guys want to come."

"I'm assuming you rich bitches are buying?" Tom questioned, wiping the sleep from his eyes.

"We can handle that," Annie said, yanking the blanket down to expose the naked bodies beneath it. "Wow."

Blake adjusted his semi as the girls looked at him appreciatively.

"Lucky you," the girl in the middle said, winking at Tom.

Blake considered telling them that he and Tom hadn't fucked but reached for the boxer briefs he'd discarded a couple of hours before.

"Maybe soon," Tom chuckled, climbing out of bed. "Are you into a free meal and some good company, Blake?"

"Yeah, sure," Blake said as he searched the floor for the rest of his clothes.

Annie tossed him his shirt. "Here you go."

"Thanks. How are you so awake after all that vodka?" he asked.

"A good amount of cocaine," she replied with a laugh. "It does wonders for perking me up."

Blake nodded. It was becoming more obvious by the moment that he was hanging out with a wild crowd. Regardless of how much fun they seemed to be, he didn't want to get sucked back into his bad habits or create new ones. Still, he was interested in finding out more about the girls' job and if Tom was into camming, too.

The chance to get paid while showing his body in front of an anonymous audience was appealing. He was in good shape and had a big dick; he'd probably be able to pull in enough cash to pay off Mr. Dennison and then some. Though Blake didn't tell the breakfast table full of new friends how interested he was in getting into camera shows, he did casually pick their brains, trying to decide if it was something he would be successful in. By the end of the meal, he was convinced that camming was a path he wanted to take, but unsure how he could get his hands on a computer. Glancing at Tom as he took his last sip of coffee, Blake had an idea, but he knew it would only work out if he made the other guy believe it was his. Luckily, he had a way with words.

32

Planting seeds in Tom's head about camming during their near-nightly drunken make out sessions had worked in Blake's favor. When Tom presented *his* brilliant idea that they should do shows together and rake in the cash, Blake was relieved. He listened intently as the other man regurgitated the bits and bobs of information he'd brought up sporadically. While he could have been forthcoming about his interest in giving the medium a go, Blake felt weird about it. They'd only known each other for a week, and, oddly enough, their hangouts hadn't escalated beyond drinking, kissing, and passing out in Tom's bed. Proposing that they should mess around on camera seemed like a big step over a thin line, and though Blake wasn't sure shit with Tom would ever be anything more than fun, he didn't want to be the one to go there.

"So, what goal do you think we should start with?" Tom asked, holding his notepad and pen at the ready.

"Do you really need to write this down?" Blake laughed. "I mean, we're doing three goals. I think we can remember."

"I've killed so many brain cells over the last few years that I don't trust the others not to stage a revolt. I have to get ahead of them."

"Oh yeah, that makes sense," Blake said sarcastically, wondering if Tom had a point. He was smart, but forgetful as fuck. "The girls said to always start with shirts off. We can do 1500 tokens for shirts. We should be able to get that, don't you think?"

"Who knows?" Tom shrugged. "They have boobs. Guys can walk around topless in public and nobody gives a shit, but they make girls keep those things under wraps. Maybe it's worth more to see a girl shirtless than a dude."

Blake nodded. "Good point. Your remaining brain cells are compensating for the many you lost."

"That's the nicest thing you ever said to me," Tom crooked, leaning over to give Blake a peck. "Kissing."

"Are we narrating what we're doing now?" Blake smirked. "I'll do it, too." He narrowed his eyes at the brunet. "Looking at you incredulously."

"Even your stink-face is hot," Tom sighed. "I'm saying it should be our second goal. A couple rounds of dirty kissing."

"Dirty kissing?"

"Lots of tongue, some lip biting. The good stuff."

"We can do that," Blake agreed, looping an arm around Tom's slim waist to pull him closer. Dress rehearsal.

Once their lips were raw and tingling from the fervent session, it was back to business.

"And what about the third goal?" Tom prompted. "Shirtless, kissing, and then..."

"We could get naked, hard, and make-out," Blake offered, not wanting to suggest what he really thought would make great content —Tom blowing him.

"There's no way I'm whipping my dick out next to yours," Tom protested. "No way. Mine will look like a thumb."

"Oh c'mon," Blake laughed, shaking his head. "If it makes you uncomfortable I could just shove mine in your ass and solve the problem."

"I bet that would be a lot more comfortable."

"Are you a virgin?" Blake asked, surprised by the possible confession.

"No, but I never fucked a horse before."

Blake punched Tom in the arm playfully. "I'm all man."

"You may be too much man for me," Tom admitted. "I should top you."

Blake pursed his lips. "I'm not really versatile."

"And by not really you mean..."

"Not at all," Blake confirmed.

"Not at all," Tom repeated, as if he was processing the information.

"Did you miss how I selected 'top' on my Rise and Grind profile? Because I promise you, it was right there. I'm cool not doing anything if you aren't into it. We can keep doing what we're doing."

"I didn't miss it. Your dick is intimidating, that's all."

"Is that why we haven't fucked?"

"No, we haven't fucked because you haven't tried to fuck," Tom stated. "If you had tried to fuck we would've fucked."

"Really?" Blake asked, floored by the admission.

"Sure, why not?"

"Well, maybe we should tease it in this show. Get people invested, and then fuck for the first time on camera. I bet we'd make a stupid amount of money."

"How much do you think we can get?" Tom asked, his blue eyes lighting up at the prospect.

"I don't know. I guess it depends on how we do tonight. I say we take it really slow and build up the anticipation and then bam, take it to the next level."

"Bam, huh?" Tom chuckled. "I'm down. I would've done it for free, but I'd rather do it for money."

Blake smiled. Suddenly, whatever had been building between them was pushed to the back burner in favor of a promise of cash. As much as he anticipated taking things to the next level, he was looking forward to the potential monetary gain more. Blake had never thought of sex in such a transactional way before, but BodyBanter was a business, and they had to approach it that way. "We can do it for money and for free."

"I like it," Tom decided. "We're on that mogul shit."

"I don't know if we can be considered moguls if we haven't made a dime."

"We're about to make a few."

Blake shrugged. He'd done enough research to know that women out earned men on camera shows the same way they did in traditional porn. While he wasn't convinced that they'd earn as much as Annie, Sophia, and Beth did, he was hopeful that they'd make more than he did in a night at the Tulip Tree Tavern. "So, are we doing this or what?" he asked, gesturing to the laptop sitting idle on the dresser.

"Yes. Let's take a couple more shots and then it's go-time," Tom said, filling the glasses he'd placed on the nightstand with cheap vodka. He downed one instantly before refilling it and giving Blake his.

It was difficult to tell if Tom was drinking to wash away the nerves or if it was his typical imbibing. Tom and the girls partied hard. Their propensity to get royally wrecked reminded Blake of Nick. Thoughts of his former friend's incarceration had him turning down the next shot Tom had tried thrust into his hand.

"I'm good," Blake assured, crossing the room to grab the computer. "I'll set it up." He placed the laptop at the foot of the bed and logged onto the website. After adjusting the tilt of the screen, he looked at Tom, who nodded his head.

And then they were live.

"Hello," Blake said smiling at the tiny lens on the top of the computer. "Welcome to our show. I'm Blake," he turned to Tom as indication that he should introduce himself, and when he didn't, he filled in, "and this is Tom."

"Look," Tom directed, pointing at the number of users in the room. Twenty-three. He dropped his voice low. "There are actually people watching."

"That's what we want," Blake whispered back. He leaned closer to the screen to see the questions and comments trickling in. "Are we a couple? No, we're not. We're friends."

"Do we want to be a couple?" Tom read with a laugh. "Uh, I don't know. We're cool with how things are, I think."

"Minus the fact that we haven't fucked," Blake added.

"Yeah, we were just talking about that," Tom told the screen. "We want to, but we haven't. It's weird."

"Super weird," Blake confirmed, placing his hand on Tom's knee.

A loud "cha-ching" from the speaker took them by surprise.

"Oh wow, SixTNine, thanks for the tip."

"We're officially official now," Tom said, holding his thumbs up. "Thanks."

"We should probably set a few goals," Blake stated, recalling the steps Annie walked him through earlier that day. "There."

"Fifty-four people," Tom noted. "Hi, everyone. Feel free to ask us questions."

Blake watched as a wall of text appeared in the chat. "Are we virgins?"

"No," Tom chuckled. "We're not. We just haven't fucked around with each other."

"BigBoy23 asks, where are we from? We're from Kentucky, BigBoy."

"Do we want to fuck?" They looked at one another and smiled. "Yeah, we want to fuck."

Cha-ching, cha-ching, cha-ching. The statement had the tips rolling in.

"That won't be for a few more shows, though. We're taking things slow," Blake informed, enunciating the last word, while making a silly face. "Really, really, *really* sexy and slow."

Cha-ching.

Tom turned to Blake. "Check it out. We're nearing our first goal. It seems like we're going to be taking our shirts off soon."

"Sounds good to me. It's getting kind of warm in here anyway."

Cha-ching, cha-ching.

"BoneTown says, 'I'll help you out,'" Tom read. "Thanks for the tip, BoneTown. Do you guys want Blake to give you a little peek at his abs? They're insane."

Compliantly, Blake lifted the hem of his t-shirt enough to show the muscles above the hem of his waistband.

Cha-ching, cha-ching.

Goal met.

As Blake yanked off his top, he grinned at the camera just as he would to a lover he was about to fuck. It came naturally. The fact that strangers were interested in seeing his body—and willing to pay money for the opportunity—made Blake horny. It was nice to be wanted and even better for that want to be backed up by funds that could eventually get him into a better place, both fiscally and emotionally. He felt a certain sense of pride that he'd taken the bull by the horns and tried something new. While he was sure Body-Banter wasn't as universally accepted as his job at the restaurant, Blake welcomed the day his wrists would ache from jacking off rather than digging into vats of ice cream. He masturbated anyway. What was the big deal of doing it onscreen?

Fleeting thoughts of his family, and their reactions if they ever found out about his most recent venture, flitted through Blake's mind, but he pushed them away. He'd attempted to live tens of lives before and was compelled to finally live his own.

The continual chime of the virtual register assured him that he was on the right track.

33

L ess than a handful of camera shows had yielded Blake enough money to pay off Mr. Dennison and then some. Though he wasn't exactly rolling in cash yet, he'd earned enough to purchase a new pair of shoes and some fresh jeans. He couldn't remember the last time he'd gone to a store and purchased clothing. Since leaving home, he'd been meticulous about caring for his stuff, knowing that he wouldn't be able to afford replacements. He knew he should be careful about his spending considering the income was variable and the medium unproven, but fuck if it didn't feel good to treat himself a bit.

As tentative as he was about the longevity of his cam career, Blake was confident that his next show was going to do well. He and Tom had built up a loyal following of people who were highly anticipating their exploration of one another. Somehow, the authenticity had translated to the screen and the viewers couldn't get enough.

Greg (11:34am): I watched you on cam yesterday.

Blake (11:37am): You watch guys' cam shows?

Greg (11:37am): Not really, but I watched yours.

Blake (11:37am): How did you come across my room if you don't search guys' shows?

Greg (11:38am): We were texting and you said you needed to go because you were getting on cam, super sleuth. Don't quit your day job.

Blake (11:39am): Oh yeah. So you watched it?

Greg (11:39am): Yup.

Blake (11:39am): That's kinda weird.

Greg (11:40am): Is it?

Blake (11:40am): I don't know...maybe! Was it weird for you?

Greg (11:40am): A little weird.

Blake (11:41am): Don't watch this afternoon.

Greg (11:41am): Now that you said that, I think I have to watch. What's happening this afternoon?

Blake (11:42am): You didn't hear our announcement at the end of the last show?

Greg (11:42am): No. I didn't watch the whole thing. I bugged out when you started to go down on him.

Blake (11:43am): Why watch it if you're not going to stick around for the end? It's the

best part.

Greg (11:43am): I'll stay for the end today.

Blake (11:43am): I told you not to watch today.

Greg (11:43am): Right, but I rarely listen to you and the fact that you're telling me not to watch makes me want to watch.

Blake (11:43am): Fine then watch.

Greg (11:44am): What's happening today?

Blake (11:44am): I'm gonna fuck Tom.

Greg (11:44am): In the ass?

Blake (11:44am): Right in the ass.

Greg (11:45am): Cool, cool.

Blake (11:45am): If you watch you better tip. It's proper etiquette.

Greg (11:45am): King of anal etiquette.

Blake (11:46am): Ha

Greg (11:46am): Can you bill me later? I'll buy you a hot dog or something and we can call it even.

Blake (11:47am): That hot dog better be wrapped in money, bitch.

Greg (11:47am): That would be dirty. Cash is filthy.

Blake (11:47am): Ok whatever. I have to get ready.

Greg (11:48am): How do you get ready?

Blake (11:48am): I don't know. I just don't feel like talking to you anymore.

Greg (11:49am): Legit. See you soon.

Blake (11:49am): That's a little creepy.

Greg (11:49am): Muahaha.

Laughing, Blake tossed his phone onto Tom's bed and knocked on the bathroom door. "How's it going?"

"Seriously?" Tom huffed.

"Yeah, I'm just asking. How much longer do you think it'll take?"

"However long it takes."

"I want to tweet a countdown or something to get people logged in as soon as we get on. Build anticipation."

"I'll tell you when you can put out a ten-minute announcement, alright?" Tom conceded.

"Okay, but how long do you think it will be until I can announce that?" Blake pressed.

"Blake!"

"What?" He tapped a lively melody onto the door. "I'm excited."

"To fuck me or to make bank?" Tom laughed.

"Both equally," Blake promised. "How much do you think we're going to pull in?"

"Can I talk to you about this when I'm done?"

"When you're done we'll be on cam. We can't talk about how much money we're making while we're making money. That would be tacky."

"And talking to me while I'm douching isn't?" Tom retorted.

"Touché," Blake laughed, leaving Tom alone to go lay on the bed. He fanned his fingers on his chest, waiting. While he'd never considered himself impatient, something about the impending show had him on pins and needles. He felt like he was on the precipice of big things, like it was the beginning of the rest of his life. Picking up his phone to distract himself, Blake found his mind was on one-track. He opened Twitter and drafted a few possible tweets, whispering the words aloud to figure out which option sounded better.

"Go ahead," Tom called.

Within seconds, the tweet was posted, and Blake was on the floor doing a set of pushups.

"Really?" Tom chuckled as he walked into the room.

"Yes, really. I want to look jacked."

"Your body is great," Tom complimented, as he tilted his head to check Blake out.

Conscious of the attention, Blake stood up, placing his hands on Tom's butt to yank him in close. "You're so hot," he crooned, slotting their mouths together as he kneaded his ass cheeks.

Though Blake wasn't sure shit would ever get serious between them, he couldn't deny that he and Tom had amazing chemistry.

"Alright," Tom said, peeling their lips apart. "I gotta go get prepped."

"I thought that was what you just did." He watched as Tom cut lines of cocaine on top of his dresser. "Oh, like that."

"I'd offer, but I know you're not into it."

The amount of drugs Tom had been doing directly correlated to the money they'd begun to earn. It was hard to tell if Tom was getting high to perform on camera or if he was deeper into the drugs because he could afford them. The more cash, the more coke, and while Blake understood the desire to get fucked up and not worry about funding it, he was beyond messing with anything but weed and alcohol.

Blake tsked. "Thanks anyway. You have condoms, right?"

"Don't you think that would have been a good thing to ask me before you came over today?" Tom questioned, rolling his tongue under his top lip.

"Do you not?"

"I do. They're in my bedside table."

"Why are you giving me shit then?" Blake chided, pulling the condoms and lube out of the drawer.

"I love giving you shit," Tom shrugged. "You're so reactive."

Shaking his head, Blake noted, "You're cold, man."

"You said I was hot two minutes ago."

"You were, now you're not," Blake smirked, laughing when Tom slapped his ass. "Get them in now, because I'm about to be spanking yours."

"Oh, that's going to happen?" Tom asked, raising his eyebrows.

"I think so. You deserve a little something."

"Mmm, do I?" Tom flirted, placing his hands on Blake's face so he could pull him in for a kiss. "This is gonna be fun."

"So much fun," Blake confirmed, giving Tom one last off-camera kiss before they logged onto the website.

"Hey, hey, hey," Tom greeted, waving at the virtual audience.

"Hey there," Blake said, watching as the viewer count continued to increase. *57, 72, 95, 112.* "Wow, there are a lot of you out there today, huh? Did you hear something big was going on?" He smirked before giving Tom a peck on the cheek.

"Today's the day."

Cha-ching.

"TyeDye12 is starting us off big with five-hundred tokens. Less than a minute in and we're halfway to our 'shirtless goal,'" Tom stated. "Thanks so much for the tip, TyeDye."

170, 218, 251, 287.

"It keeps jumping up by, like, thirty," Blake whispered to Tom, who gave him a cheeky grin in reply. "Yes, MegaMan," he read the handle in the comment, "it's the day for fucking and we're both really fucking excited."

Cha-ching, cha-ching, cha-ching.

"Thanks, guys. We've definitely waited long enough," Tom confirmed. "Um," he turned to Blake, "CumSkank wants to know if you're going to split me in half."

324, 410, 444.

"Well, CumSkank, that's the plan. It's what he deserves," Blake answered, waggling his eyebrows.

"Aw, thanks, babe." Tom stole a kiss and kept his blown-out pupils locked on Blake's for a moment.

"My pleasure."

"It will be," Tom promised.

Cha-ching, cha-ching, cha-ching.

A chipper fanfare announced that they'd met the first goal.

"And just like that we're losing our shirts," Blake narrated. "Thanks, TyeDye, CumPieI, and Jacksin."

613, 692, 736.

"Are you seeing this?" Tom muttered as they took off their tops. He traced his finger down Blake's sternum before rubbing his abs.

Cha-ching, cha-ching, cha-ching.

"Yeah, this is fucking crazy," Blake replied, in awe by the way the numbers were continuously climbing. "Thanks for the tip, guys. The next goal is 'naked and hard,' one-thousand tokens. Let's get there fast. I'm ready to go."

"Me too," Tom agreed, nudging Blake with his knee and gesturing toward his vibrating phone.

Blake chuckled when he looked at the screen.

Greg (1:12pm): Pull your ear to say hi to me.

Greg (1:15pm): Don't sit there laughing, prick. Pull it.

"Fuck off, Greg," Blake joked, flipping the camera the bird.

1021, 1063, 1084.

"The people want to know if Greg's your ex," Tom said, rubbing Blake's back.

Cha-ching, cha-ching.

"No, he's my annoying friend," Blake answered. "Thanks, MegaMan and CumPieI. We're only eight-hundred away from the next goal."

Greg (1:20pm): You're annoying. Fuck you right back.

Blake rolled his eyes and tugged his ear. "There you go."

Cha-ching, cha-ching, cha-ching.

Greg (1:21pm): See how easy that was?

"TyeDye says Blake should turn off his phone. I agree, TyeDye."

"I do, too," Blake said, shutting it down. He was at work. "Seven-hundred-and-twenty to our goal."

"I'm tempted to skip the next one and go right to the banging,"

Tom flirted, licking his lips as he rubbed his palms over Blake's abs. "You look beyond sexy right now."

As they made out, Blake listened to a steady succession of tips, followed by the flourish of another goal met.

"Thanks guys," Tom said breathlessly. "We're noticing all your names, I promise, and we're super appreciative."

"Definitely," Blake agreed as he shed his pants and boxer briefs. He stood up to give the camera a view of his ready cock.

1097, 1120, 1153.

Cha-ching, cha-ching, cha-ching.

"The screen's frozen," Tom reported, attempting to refresh the page. "I think we broke it."

"Broke what?" Blake asked, leaning over to check out the screen. "BodyBanter?"

"Yeah. We're getting a server error."

"Holy shit," Blake laughed. "Do you really think it's us?"

"I really think it's us," Tom asserted, his eyes wide. "They don't have the bandwidth for the activity or something."

"The girls are going to be so pissed we're fucking up their afternoon."

"So pissed."

"What are we supposed to do?" Blake wondered.

"You can blow me while we wait."

Blake grinned and dropped to his knees.

As he serviced Tom, all he could think about was how he hoped someone was servicing the overwhelmed website. They had a show to do.

34

W hile Blake had expected the consummation cam show to be a hit, he never imagined it would be as epic as it was. Not only did they break BodyBanter, but Blake and Tom managed to make more money than Blake had made over months at the Tulip Tree Tavern. Since he kept his job at the restaurant while he was building a following, Blake was finally doing alright. It had been so long since he felt he was being compensated fairly for his work. If anything, he was awed by the chance to make money doing something he would have done anyway. He loved sex, and obviously people loved watching him have it. It was a win-win. Still, there were tough decisions to be made.

As much as Blake liked Tom, being around his lifestyle was asking for trouble. Tom was snorting an insane amount of coke now that he had a steady stream of income, and his constant use was wearing on Blake. It wasn't like he wanted to do cocaine all of sudden just because Tom was, but he struggled with his ability to control his thoughts of Adderall. It was wild that a prescription drug could have flipped the script on his life. There was no way he was going to let any substance take hold of him the way the orange powder had. So, in an effort to stay well, Blake invested in his own laptop and paid Peter and Dave's overdo cable bill, driven to go out on his own.

The majority of the comments on BodyBanter and Twitter were about Blake's assets; his body, his dick, his personality. While he was grateful to have had a partner in the beginning, he was starting to believe he could be successful on his own. And he was right. In his first solo show, Blake raked in almost as much as he made on the earlier shows with Tom. The influx of money confirmed what he'd suspected. He was the draw.

Tom had taken it relatively well. He told Blake porn had never been his goal anyway and that once he earned enough for a year of tuition he was going to quit. It wasn't until he realized Blake was ending off-camera stuff that Tom became irritated.

"So, that's it? We're not even going to fuck for fun anymore? Like, I get you wanting to veer off on your own on BodyBanter, but why can't we bang?" Tom asked, seeming completely perplexed by the turn of events.

"I think it's better if we make a clean break," Blake said, not wanting to go into great detail about how Tom's lifestyle had become a dangerous deterrent. The truth was, Blake wasn't convinced he'd want to be with the guy even if he was straight-laced and responsible. Try as he might, he couldn't get Jay off his mind.

His ex was everything he was looking for, and Blake worried nobody else would be able to stand up to his comparisons. It was a challenge to get over someone who had dug so deep under his skin. He wanted to believe it was possible, though, because if it wasn't he would feel obligated to suffer. As the months passed, Blake's belief that they'd eventually work things out had dwindled. Dave had convinced him that it was only a matter of time, but time kept passing and Jay wasn't coming around. Occasionally, Blake attempted to connect, hoping that the effort would be rewarded with a lengthy conversation. It never was.

Blake (6:25pm): Hey. I know finals are next week. I wanted to wish you luck.

Jay (6:39pm): Thanks, Blake.

"Blake." Not "baby" or "love," but his first name as if Jay hardly knew him. He'd considered what to write back in a plan to stimulate conversation, but after an array of ideas, Blake did nothing. It was too strange to be a stranger to a man who had claimed to love him. He wanted to be as far away from the heartbreak as possible. So, he traveled to Florida.

Blake was surprised when his former Facebook flame, Caden, reached out to him. It had been years since they'd last chatted online. Though they had a strong connection, time, distance, and the inability to meet in person wore on their relationship. Still, there was history between them, and the fact that Caden was also camming hinted at the chance that there was a present, too. Finally having enough money to get out of Kentucky, if even just for a couple of days, Blake boarded a plane for a long overdue date. The trip was intended to be for pleasure in more ways than one, but it turned out to be highly educational as well.

A quick Google search after checking Caden out on BodyBanter had informed Blake that his friend had parlayed his camera success into a career in porn. Caden's scenes were incredibly hot, and once Blake began his descent down the Helix Studios rabbit hole, he found that the rest of the content on their site was fire, too.

"Porn, huh?" Blake asked as he lay in bed beside Caden.

"Yup."

"Tell me about it," Blake prompted, turning on his side to have a better view of Caden's handsome face.

"There's not much to tell," Caden shrugged. "I get to fuck hot guys and it pays the bills," he paused, "and then some."

"I can see," Blake noted, glancing around Caden's bedroom. Though the place wasn't a palace, it was nice with its new furniture and top of the line speaker system.

"I'm not rolling in it, but I'm doing alright."

"How often do you film?"

"They fly me out to San Diego once a month and I do a few

scenes, lay on the beach, and party," Caden replied as he tickled Blake's arm. "It's fun."

"It sounds like fun," Blake said, his interest officially piqued. Like with all things, he knew there wasn't a chance it was as straightforward as Caden presented it to be. "There have to be downsides, though. If it was that easy and enjoyable everyone would do it."

Caden laughed at the assertion. "Dude, it's still porn. Not everyone would do it because you literally get naked and fuck on camera. It takes a certain type of person and a big set of balls."

"I mean..." Blake smirked, gesturing toward his lap, "check."

"Yeah, well, the whole world is going to see them if you decide to try to do porn. It's something you have to think about."

"First of all, the whole world doesn't watch gay porn."

"They should," Caden interrupted with a chuckle. "Imagine the good it could do for the Middle East."

"Peace, finally," Blake grinned. "Seriously though, there's no way the general public recognizes you from your scenes."

"Well, they don't, but I can't rule out the chance that someday it will bite me in the ass."

"You like having your ass bitten," Blake teased, gnashing his teeth together.

"With jobs and shit in the future," Caden admonished, playfully flicking Blake's ear. "Once it's out there, it's out there. There's no taking it back."

Blake shrugged. "The same could be said for BodyBanter."

"Yeah, but that's on a much smaller scale. Cam sites don't have the reach that the major porn companies do."

"Do your parents know you do porn?"

"Do yours know you cam?" Caden shot back.

"Deflecting skills on fleek!" Blake joked, squeezing Caden's obliques. "My dad knows but I haven't told my mom yet."

"Yet?" Caden asked, raising his eyebrows in interest. "You're going to tell her?"

"Sure, I've had to tell her way more fucked up shit in the past, at least camming is legal and I'm making money."

"What does your dad think?"

"He's a free-spirit," Blake said easily. "He thinks it's cool."

"Do you think she will?"

Blake shrugged. "I don't know. I'm still working at the Tulip Tree Tavern so it's not like there's no going back. I think my dad's glad about that."

"Your parents are way different than mine," Caden sighed. "If they ever found out they would disown me."

"Then they don't deserve you," Blake stated.

"That's simple to say but when you're facing it, it's a lot more complicated."

"Why did you do it then? Porn. Why'd you do it if you thought there was a chance you wouldn't be able to handle the ramifications?"

"Because it's fun," Caden grinned, "and I'm only young once, right? I want to live life to its fullest and deal with consequences as they come."

"And you think they'll come?"

"They always come," Caden answered with a wink.

"Do they?" Blake laughed, rolling on top of Caden to slot their mouths together.

As they kissed, Blake reminded himself that although Caden was sexy, he wasn't the kind of guy he needed long-term. He was a worry-about-the-consequences-later kind of guy, and Blake needed a guy who weighed the consequences before making a decision, someone who would make him better. Someone like Jay. Time spent with other people seemed to do nothing but confirm to Blake that he wanted to be with his ex. Unfortunately, wanting to be with someone and having the ability to actually be with them wasn't the same. Longing didn't promise fulfillment, no matter how much the satisfaction was craved. Intent on pushing the swirl of thoughts from his mind, Blake decided to push a finger inside of Caden.

"Mmm," Caden crooned, climbing on top of him. "I wanna ride you."

"Go ahead then," Blake grinned.

Placing his hands behind his head, Blake decided there was no use in worrying about things he couldn't control, especially if he could lay back and enjoy giving it up to someone else. At least for a night.

35

Though Blake prided himself on having an abundance of pride, he wasn't too prideful to contact Jay when he returned home from Florida. It had been too long since they had last seen each other, and Blake was convinced that if he could just get in front of him they could work things out. He wasn't wrong.

"I missed you," Blake whispered into Jay's neck as he fucked him.

"Holy shit," Jay sighed, throwing his head back on the pillow, his fingernails digging into Blake's flexing back muscles. "I missed you, too."

"This or me?" Blake asked breathlessly, the distinction important to him, even in the heat of their passion.

As soon as Blake entered Jay's apartment their lips had been on one another, and it had taken seconds for their bodies to follow suit. While his intention had been for them to speak, Blake couldn't deny that reconnecting physically was pretty fucking nice. Though Blake had banged a bunch of people after they'd broken up, the sex was better with someone he loved.

"Both," Jay confessed.

The admission brought a wide smile to Blake's face. Jay missed him just like he'd missed Jay. They were having sex and they'd missed each other. He liked his odds of a longer-term reunion.

Falling into a familiar rhythm, they worked toward climax and shuddered their way down as they kissed hungrily. They snuck glances and grins as they pulled apart, lying on the pillow beside each other.

"So," Blake began, rubbing his knuckles against the scruff on Jay's chin. "That was amazing."

"It always is," Jay agreed, holding Blake's hand so he could give it a smooch. "I'm glad you're here."

"I'm glad to be here. It's just like old times."

"It's only been a couple of months."

"It feels like years ago," Blake mused.

"What have you been up to?" Jay wondered, squeezing Blake's bicep. "Other than working out."

"I haven't been working out that much. I sort of got into a new business venture that's taking up my time."

"Sort of? How can you be successful at something if you're only sort of into it?" Jay challenged.

Blake had debated whether he should tell Jay about his foray into BodyBanter. He wasn't sure if it was a good idea to do so, but the intimacy of the moment inspired him to be forthcoming.

"I guess I'm dipping my toes in, feeling the temperature or whatever."

"Are you speaking in codes? What are you up to?" Jay asked, scrunching his nose up in skepticism.

Blake purposely scrunched back, garnering an eye roll and a chuckle from his ex.

"C'mon. Spit it out," Jay urged. "You've got me curious."

"Isn't it fun to keep a little mystery?" Blake suggested, giving him a cheeky grin.

"What? No." Jay shook his head for emphasis. "You're the one who brought it up and now you're going to try to back out of it?"

"I'm second-guessing this revelation," Blake admitted, feeling every bit of his regret as it formed a lump in his throat.

"What did you get yourself into?" Jay questioned, his eyes wide.

"What do you think I got myself into?"

"I have no idea, but the way you're acting leads me to believe it's something shady as hell. Are you dealing?"

"Drugs?" Blake cried. "Am I dealing drugs?"

"What do you think I mean, cards? Yes, drugs."

"I'm not dealing drugs," he huffed.

"Okay, what is it then?" Jay pressed, adjusting his position so he could get a better view of Blake's face.

"Have you ever heard of BodyBanter?"

"No."

"Well, it's this website where you can either watch people do shows or you can do shows yourself and earn tips for different things you do."

"I'm guessing from the name of the site that these shows are sex shows?"

"They could be," Blake nodded, studying Jay's eyes for a reaction. There was nothing. "Some people just strip, fuck around with a dildo, get into fetish shit, you know, whatever they're into. Like there are rooms where people just show their feet for an hour, maybe rub them, put lotion on, that kind of thing."

"And is that what you're doing?" Jay wondered, licking his lips. "Massaging your feet on camera for an hour?"

"No, I'm not doing anything with my feet."

"What are you doing then?"

"You know what I'm doing," Blake tsked, gently tickling the soft skin of Jay's belly. "You want me to say it?"

"Why are you doing it if you can't even say it?"

Blake bristled at the implication that he was ashamed of his endeavor. "I can say it. I'm doing cam shows."

"By yourself?"

"Sometimes."

"And other times?"

"Not by myself," Blake said plainly.

Jay sniffed and nudged his thumb against his nostril. "Hmm."

"Does that bother you?" Blake asked, though it was obvious it did.

"That you do it at all or that you do it with other people?"

"I guess, either?"

"It's a lot to take in," Jay confessed.

"That's what you said five minutes ago, too," Blake teased, lifting his eyebrows. "Huh, huh." He poked Jay in the ribs playfully. "C'mon, that's funny."

"It would be funny if I actually complained about it," Jay teased.

"This size queen!" Blake laughed, kissing Jay's smiling lips. "Seriously, though. I'm making good money doing it. Between that income and the Tulip Tree Tavern, I'm earning more than I ever have."

"Really?" Jay asked, surprised.

"Really. It's amazing. I can go on whenever I want to rake in some cash. We could go on now..." he flirted.

"Yeah right," Jay chuckled. "That's never happening."

"I make the same amount doing shows by myself anyway."

"Have you done a lot of shows with other guys?" Jay asked, cringing through the question.

"We were broken up," Blake reminded.

"We still are."

"I don't want to be."

"You're avoiding my question," Jay noted.

"I've only gone on cam with two guys. One I met after you dumped me and the other, Caden, I've known for a while through Facebook. We finally met in person last week. He's into camming, too."

"Why did it take you so long to meet in person?"

"He's in Florida."

"He came to Kentucky to do a show with you?"

"I went there."

"Wow," Jay exclaimed.

Blake draped his arm over Jay's chest. Not only did he want to feel closer to him, but he wanted to give him a semblance of comfort. "Does that bother you?"

"It doesn't matter if it does."

"It matters to me," Blake reassured. "Are you jealous?"

"I guess."

"You ended things with me."

"That doesn't mean I stopped caring," Jay said softly, pushing a lock of hair off Blake's forehead.

"You had a funny way of showing it."

"I'm sorry. It felt like the right thing to do at the time."

"Does it now?"

"Not really," Jay sighed, intertwining their fingers. "I miss you."

"I miss you," Blake promised. "Did you at least do well last semester?"

"I got a 4.0."

"It was worth it then."

Jay shook his head. "I don't think so."

"Bullshit, you did well, which is exactly what you wanted. Dave told me you'd want to get back together after school was done."

"Who said I wanted to get back together?"

"Do you not? I thought that's what this was leading to?" Blake asked, confused.

"I thought I did."

"And now you don't? Is it the cam stuff?"

Taking a deep breath, Jay loosened his hold of Blake's hand. "I don't want to tell you what you can and can't do, or give you an ultimatum. I can tell you're excited about it, but I can't deal with you hooking up with other guys."

"So I won't," Blake said easily. "I told you, I make a good amount on my own. If you're cool with me doing it solo, then I'll do that."

"You'd be cool with no more shows with your Florida boy?"

"He's my Florida boy now?" Blake chuckled. "I'm fine not doing more shows with Caden. He's moving on from camming and I'm moving on from camming with other dudes."

"And girls..." Jay added.

"And girls."

"What's he moving on to?"

"He does porn."

"You do, too," Jay asserted.

Blake shook his head. "Actual porn with a studio and stuff."

"Oh. You know, this is a conversation I didn't foresee myself having today," Jay admitted. "It feels," he paused, clearly attempting to choose his words carefully, "far from what I consider normal, you know?"

"I get it," Blake confirmed.

"That's not something you want to do, right? Like, you're not looking to eventually sign with a studio, are you?"

"No," Blake stated. "Caden mentioned that one of the producers watched our cam show and was interested in me, but I haven't talked to anyone about anything."

"But would you?"

It was a difficult question, and one that had crossed Blake's mind. The amount of money he was making on BodyBanter couldn't compare to the porn wages Caden had divulged. Although Blake had never given it serious consideration, he'd been viewing Helix's scenes differently than he had previously. He no longer jacked off watching. Instead, he studied them closer, as though he'd eventually be tested on the content. He figured if anything, it would make him better on cam.

"I just told you I wouldn't go on cam with other people, I figured your request went for porn, too," Blake reasoned.

"Well, it does, but I don't want to stop you from doing something you want to do."

"Who said I want to do it? I don't."

"Really?" Jay asked, skeptically.

"Really," Blake confirmed, taking Jay's hand. "Are we going to try again?"

"I'd like to."

"Are you going to dump me in the fall when school starts up again?"

"No. I think I freaked out. I was feeling these strong emotions I've never felt before, and it was consuming me. I needed some time to reflect and get my shit together," Jay reassured him.

"And is it together?"

"Yeah."

"You blindsided me," Blake reminded.

"I know. I'm sorry."

"If you start worrying about things like that, I want you to tell me, not just freak out."

"Fair," Jay nodded. "I will."

"Now get up on there and ride your boyfriend," Blake requested biting his tongue playfully, while gesturing to his hard-on.

Jay eagerly complied.

36

T
hroughout the course of his adolescence, Blake had never felt that he belonged in one particular place. His roots had spread far and wide, leading him to new schools, different groups of friends, and an unceasing succession of beginnings that ended too soon. Since change had been his constant, he resisted the urge to burrow in it, knowing it would only be a matter of time until the iota of a grasp he managed was obliterated by the bulldozer of life. There was no glory in his ability to adapt because he'd had no choice but to do so. To celebrate acclimation was acknowledging an empty victory, like exalting himself for taking a piss or brushing his teeth.

Blake had grown used to the way people cycled in and out of his life, and how he was rarely a steady presence in theirs. However, it always seemed that the most important figures found their way back. From his father to Sandra, Ryan, Bianca and even Caden, there was a certain comfort in their return, like a homecoming not contained by the walls of a house. He wondered if his feelings were unique to him or if everyone felt them to some extent. Were there people whose lives were full of Gregs? Who had the luck of having ride-or-die family, friends, and lovers? As much as Blake hoped Jay would become a constant, the sucker-punch dumping remained in the back of his mind, a reminder that it could happen again.

Still, the summer was submersed in contentedness. Blake continued to work nights at the Tulip Tree Tavern, but Jay's availability during the day allowed for uninterrupted hours spent drinking Corona at the community pool in Jay's complex or in bed, where they relished in the air conditioning as they brought the heat. The following Blake built for his camera shows created a second income as steady as what he earned at the diner. Everything was both amazing and unremarkable, a surprisingly copacetic combination. Though it was nice to live his new status quo, Blake was antsy, so used to perpetual erraticism that the calm felt odd. He compelled himself to relish it, knowing how quickly a whispered secret, a car crash, or any misstep could alter the trajectory of his life. He hadn't expected a simple phone call to be the impetus for the most intense change yet.

"Hey."

"Blake?" Caden asked tentatively.

"Of course it is," Blake laughed. You called me, Caden." Jay's recognition of the name had him regarding Blake curiously. "How are you?"

"Good. I haven't heard from you since you left Florida. It's been a while, man."

"I haven't heard from you either," Blake retorted, standing up from the couch where he'd been sitting beside Jay to take the call in his boyfriend's bedroom. "What's going on?"

"Not much. I've been filming a lot. I signed an exclusive, so work's been steady."

"Awesome, and you're still enjoying it?" Blake asked, lying on the bed and adjusting the pillow so it was comfortably cradling his head.

"There's not much not to enjoy. I get paid to screw hot guys," Caden reasoned. "I don't know what could be better than that."

"You told me there were some cons to the whole thing," he reminded, recalling the short list of concerns Caden had shared about his career.

"Honestly, I can't see them beyond the money," Caden chuckled.

"It's that good?"

"Yeah. It's not like they throw it at you but there are a lot of oppor-tunities besides the actual filming."

"Appearances and stuff?"

"You got it," Caden confirmed.

"Damn. That's cool."

"It is. Do you still have your restaurant job or are you just camming?"

"I'm doing both."

"So, the camming money hasn't been good?" Caden questioned.

"It's great," Blake bristled. "What are you angling at?"

"Nothing," he replied quickly. "It's been months and people haven't stopped talking about our cam show, including my bosses."

"Oh yeah? They're saying shit about it to you?" Blake asked, stunned by the revelation. While he knew his followers were into him, he never imagined that he would remain on the minds of men who spent their days around the hottest guys. Blake had never had confidence issues, but there was nothing like a good stroke to the ego, and Caden was working it well.

"All the time."

"You're exaggerating," Blake accused.

"Maybe a little bit, but it doesn't take away from the fact that they were intrigued by you."

"Intrigued, huh?" Blake repeated. "They're intrigued by me? Why?"

"Your personality, looks, cock..." Caden said as though it should be entirely obvious. "Have you given any thought to applying?"

"I mean, I think about it, but it's not like I'm hardcore considering it or anything."

"Why not?"

It was a good question. Since getting back together with Jay, Blake didn't let his mind get lost in scenarios where he exploited the popu-larity and the success he'd found on BodyBanter. It was enough to make money on his own terms and he didn't look beyond the present.

But, sometimes, despite his efforts, Blake would shift to a more curious state where his resistance would wane. He would find himself perusing the Helix website once again, wondering if he had the wherewithal to take the step, and if Jay would ever be open to the idea to walk beside him as he did. It was too much to ask of someone, so he stopped asking himself if it was an option, even when he wanted to know the answer.

"Why am I not considering it?" Blake mused. "Um, a bunch of reasons."

"Do you care to share any of them?" Caden pressed. His demeanor was much more supportive than pressure-laden, like he was trying to set caged potential free.

"Well, for one, my boyfriend is against it."

"Boyfriend." Caden declared, as if the word itself was an insult. "Since when?"

"A few months."

"Oh."

"Yeah."

They were silent for a moment, the awkward exchange robbing them both of words.

"I didn't think you expected anything," Blake said, finally. "I thought it was for a purpose, you know?"

"And that's why you'd be good in porn," Caden asserted. "Because you're able to separate the act from the emotion."

"Are you saying I'm cold?"

"I'm saying you're perfect," Caden stated. "I don't know. It's something to think about. You have the opportunity if you want it. All you have to do is apply."

He made it sound simple. As if filling out an application and sending pictures wouldn't affirm the decision Blake feared he would make. As if when the opportunity was tangible, he would have the ability to turn away from it and remain in Jay's arms. He loved his boyfriend, but temptation was a motherfucker. There was no reason to dangle himself in front of it, especially when he wasn't sure his ropes would hold.

"You really like it?" Blake asked cautiously, tip-toeing around the answer he already knew. He wanted to hear it again.

"I love it," Caden promised. "I'm not trying to talk you into anything. I want you to know you have the chance. That's it."

"Well, I appreciate you reaching out," Blake said, peeking up at Jay, who was leaning on the frame of the door. Waving him in, Blake welcomed him under his arm as he wrapped up the conversation with Caden. "Thanks for thinking of me."

"No problem, Blake. I hope you'll consider it. I think you'd be great."

"Thanks. I'll talk to you later."

"Later."

Ending the call, Blake tossed his phone onto the bed beside him. "What are you thinking for dinner? Do you think we should warm up some of Jane's world-famous mac and cheese?"

"What was that about?" Jay asked, looking up at Blake with his dark blue eyes.

"You have the nicest eyelashes," Blake commented, tapping the pad of his finger against the long lashes. "Has anyone told you that before?"

"Has anyone told you it's obvious when you're avoiding a subject you don't want to talk about?"

"You have. Several times," Blake smirked, letting out a labored sigh when Jay didn't smile back.

"Be honest with me."

"I'm always honest with you."

"Okay. I'm waiting then," Jay said, sitting up and guiding Blake by the wrist to do the same. They sat facing each other, Blake wondering why the air in the room was suddenly so thick. He coughed through the constriction.

"I guess a few of Caden's producers are really interested in me."

"Romantically?" Jay asked, confused.

"No, no. Interested in me coming to work for them. Caden pretty much told me if I apply it'll be a done deal."

"What gave them the impression that you'd be interested? Did you submit something?"

"I didn't submit anything," Blake promised. "They really liked the show I did with Caden in Florida."

"That was a while ago."

"They think I have a lot of potential," Blake shrugged.

"And what do you think?" Jay wondered.

"I know I have potential. That's not the issue."

"What's the issue? Me?" Jay asked, rolling his lips in tight.

"No! Why would you ever say that?" Blake chided, taking both of his boyfriend's hands in his. "You could never be an issue."

"I told you I didn't want to stand in your way if you wanted to do the porn thing."

"Who said I want to do it?"

"You did."

"I never said that," Blake asserted. "Not once."

"You never said it with words," Jay agreed, "but you sure as hell say it in your actions. You don't even jerk off when you go on the website. You get this faraway look in your eyes like you're daydreaming. You randomly mention the business whenever you have a chance to bring it up. You kill it on BodyBanter every time you log on. Fuck, that even has me thinking if taking your career further is a good option for you."

"You think about it?" Blake asked, shocked by the statement. "Really?"

"Really," Jay confirmed. "I can tell it's something you want."

"So, you know me better than I know myself?" Blake snarked. "You're telling me what I want now?"

"I love you," Jay said simply. "I don't want to stand in the way of what you want to do, of something you'd be successful with."

"Who said you were?"

"I told you I couldn't be with you if you did porn."

"And has your position changed?" Blake ventured, admonishing himself for the amount of hope that seeped into his voice.

"My position hasn't changed," Jay said, regretfully.

"Well, that's good, because mine hasn't either. I'm not interested."

"You're lying."

"Why are you pushing this?" Blake sighed, dropping Jay's hand. "What do you want me to do?"

"I want you to do what makes you happy."

"*You* make me happy," Blake promised. "You, this apartment, this summer, this life. That's what makes me happy."

"I love you."

"I love you, too."

"I don't want to hold you back," Jay continued, resting his palm on Blake's cheek.

He leaned into the touch. "You aren't. It's not like that."

"If you think it's what's best for you, I want you to do it."

"Are we still talking about porn?" Blake scoffed, opening his eyes abruptly. "Really? Like, we're seriously talking about porn being what's best for me?"

"I mean, it's not a conversation I ever foresaw myself having," Jay admitted, "but here we are."

"Right," Blake nodded. "I'm here with you, not doing porn, not thinking about porn. I'm not thinking about any of this shit. I'm thinking about how fucking badly I want a big plate of Jane's macaroni and cheese," he ranted, standing up and stomping into the kitchen. "And how much I don't want to talk about this anymore," he yelled for good measure.

So, they didn't talk about it, until eventually, they did.

EPILOGUE

Three days after Jay mercy-dumped him, Blake sent his photos to Helix Studios. Twenty-four hours later, they emailed him a plane ticket to San Diego. Staring at his phone screen, he felt a swell of joy he hadn't expected. Jay was right, Blake wanted it more than he was willing to admit. Enough to understand Jay's intention when he once again broke up with him. Though it hurt, Jay gave him the gift of possibility, a chance Blake never would have taken at the expense of their relationship. Jay let him go because Blake wouldn't leave on his own, and though it pained him, Blake was thankful. Without the push he would've remained happy but stagnant, something he was never comfortable being. He needed more, and Jay loved him enough to make him chase it, even if they both had a hard time believing that Blake's *more* was a career most considered obscene.

It wasn't that way to Blake. Although he stopped short of thinking his cam shows bettered people's lives, he did know he enhanced them. He'd chatted with enough of his followers to understand that they were from different walks of life and varied circumstances. While some of them were lonely, others weren't, using the medium to spice up their relationships or get lost in a fantasy. Not only did heating up other people's sex lives make him feel good, it also turned him on. He often wondered how many orgasms his viewers had along with him. How much pleasure he brought to another person simply by pleasuring himself. There was so much suffering in the world; to provide positive moments of release to fans who needed them was awesome.

Growing up, Blake thought he was more like his mother than his father, but his adulthood had taught him that his assumption was wrong. His dad had always been an enigma, a man who spread love while not giving enough at home. Blake never got it when he was young, how his father could care about him and Logan if he was in and out of their lives. The older he got, the more Blake realized that some people were meant to move, to share with too many and be understood by too few. The things he'd never accepted about his father were the same ones he'd been forced to acknowledge in himself. He couldn't be everything to anyone, but he could be something to everyone. Maybe he'd never be enough to the people who mattered, but he couldn't worry about that, there was so much more to focus on.

He'd spent years avoiding Uniontown. Turning down his mother's invitations because he couldn't stand the idea of being in a town full of people who ruined him. As soon as his mother pulled her car onto a familiar country road, Blake was plagued by thoughts of Jeremiah Burbar, Steve Cooks and the other assholes on the wrestling team whose prejudice made his life hell. The fields were orange with Adderall, the same color as the jumpsuit Nick Holgate would pull on and off for the rest of his life, a hue Blake vowed to avoid. The shade trees that hovered over the car as it drove down the street were Xander Marks and Claire's family, people who judged him because he wanted something they didn't want him to want, be it girls or boys. To them, he would never make the right choice. They didn't understand that there wasn't one. It wasn't one or the other, it never had been.

"Are you okay?" Grace asked, patting Blake's knee as she drove.

"Why wouldn't I be?" he replied, too embarrassed to admit that he was anything but. The smartest thing he'd done over the last couple of years was avoid Uniontown. The deluge of emotions wasn't worth the effort, even if it made his mom happy. He didn't know why she cared about having him at the house anyway. They had a great time when she visited Lexington. Her insistence that he come home, even just for a couple of hours, was like her torture. He couldn't blame her for wanting everything to be alright. Deep down, he did too, but Blake doubted he would ever find solace in a town where his life had been so turbulent.

"I'm glad you're here," she replied, biting her lip. "I want you to remember where you come from before you go away."

"What's the point of remembering this place?" Blake asked.

Though he'd never filled his mother in on all that had gone down during his days at Woodland County High School, she couldn't have been dense enough to miss the signs that things had been bad.

"Because whether you like it or not, it made you who you are, and I want you to remember who you are when you get to wherever you're going."

Blake had told Grace exactly what he would be doing in San Diego, and she seemed to cope with the news by speaking like Yoda and remaining as vague as possible. He didn't give her shit about it, though. He'd given her enough of that throughout his high school years.

"You think I should hold Kentucky values?" he scoffed, shaking his head at the suggestion. "I don't think that'll get me far in California."

"Not Kentucky values, per say, but Mitchell values, maybe. I haven't raised you to be any certain way other than smart, Blake. Be smart out there. If something doesn't feel right, it isn't. You know that, and you know how to say no."

"Of course I do," Blake promised. "It's not like that, though. It's not predatory like you're making it seem."

"And you know this how?" Grace challenged. "I'm just saying, despite everything, you have a good head on your shoulders and I want to know you're going to use it."

"I'll use it."

"You should take Greg out there with you. You're still in touch, aren't you? It may be good for you to have some moral support."

"You have time to wrap your mind to wrap around the fact that this is a good thing. I'm not scared of it, I'm not dreading it..."

"It's hard for me to imagine you doing this, Blake."

"You really shouldn't try to imagine it," Blake cringed. "Seriously, did you ever think about the sex I had with my girlfriends or boyfriends? There are just some things that parents shouldn't think about, right?"

"It makes it difficult when you're looking to have this as a career. What should I tell people? When they ask what you're up to, what should I say?"

"Who the hell is asking about me?" Blake said with a laugh.

"Sometimes the girls at the office ask me," she informed him defensively.

"You can tell them I'm at the restaurant. What do you care what they think anyway?"

"What a blessing it is for you that you don't care about other people's impressions of you!" Grace exclaimed. "I wish you got that quality from me."

"I got a lot of good qualities from you," Blake promised. "You know what you should do? Tell them to fuck off."

"Blake!"

"I'm serious. It would be liberating for you."

"Do you know what would be liberating for me?"

"I think you're about to tell me..."

"Your success. I don't want to lose sleep worrying about your future," Grace stated.

"You don't have to worry about me," Blake said. "I've been worrying about myself for a while, and I'm doing well. It may not be what you imagined for me, but this is good. It's something I need to do."

"How could I not worry about you?" Grace asked.

As she pulled into the driveway, Blake remembered pushing the blue Saturn to the street

in an attempt to avoid revving the engine and waking his mom.

"I'm different now."

"In what ways?"

"All the ones that matter," Blake stated, exiting the car the moment his mother turned off the ignition. "I'm going to go for a walk."

"We just got here," Grace tsked. "At least say hi to your brother first.

"He's not going anywhere."

"Come back soon," she relented, "Dinner's in twenty."

Blake nodded before heading on his way. Although he didn't know where he was going, he knew he needed to walk and clear his mind of oppressive thoughts. Trekking down the road, he made his way to a familiar spot. The place didn't hold much meaning to him, but it didn't stop the moment from being meaningful. He'd been there hundreds of times, but he'd never felt the way he did that day. It was as if he was seeing an old world through new eyes, an unexpected awakening. What had seemed promising in Lexington was suddenly promised in Uniontown, not because of where he was, but because of who he had become in spite of the place where he was raised.

As he stood on the hill overlooking the lush green land below, Blake was bigger than the small town that had sought to minimize him. The fear of failure that had tethered him to ideals that were never ideal for him dissipated more and more with every dollar he made doing something he enjoyed. Like the flock of birds he watched fly toward the apricot sunset, he was free. He wasn't his mistakes as he believed he was in the past. He was his future, and even in the dimming moments of the dusky hour, he was bright.

THE RISE UP SERIES

Book Two
October 2018